At Sea

A Viv Fraser Mystery

V. Clifford

Inverardoch Press

Published by Inverardoch Press

Chapter One

'Hello. Hello . . . Oh, piss off.'

Viv Fraser tossed her mobile onto the passenger seat of her Rav and started the engine. It was the third time in as many days that she'd answered and been met with silence.

Her first clients lived in East Lothian. She sighed and rolled her shoulders to relieve the strange tetchiness gnawing at the edge of her consciousness. She turned right onto the A1, leaving behind streams of traffic going into the centre of Edinburgh. An early morning frost had thawed but a slight mist still threatened her chances of a great view of the Forth estuary. This was one of her favourite journeys, especially on a morning like this, with an expanse of washed-out blue sky, and rolling farmland stretched out on either side of the long ribbon of tarmac. To her right a group of odd low-lying buildings, evidence of an influx of new light industry. Further on and to her left she noticed a few more new buildings, vast white barns, windowless, with silver solar-panelled roofs – not a chance that they'd be used for livestock. She'd read that a tech initiative had bought up a big country house to exploit its parkland and barns but their planning application for a 'science park' had been turned down despite the fact they'd already invested in a new slip road, its purpose known only to those who worked there or had been invited. Such discreet signage was surely an oxymoron. Whether she imagined it or not she believed she could smell the sea. She opened the windows on the passenger side of the Rav and drank in the fresh air. Being a morning person was all very well until morning began the night before. Another sleepless night and too much time online had left her fuzzy-headed. Yet another silent call hadn't helped.

Her destination was an extensive old farm, its lands overlooked by a hilltop monument dedicated to an Earl of Wemyss. The current generation, her clients, had inherited a working arable farm but it had gradually become more of a stud for breeding horses, with many fields turned to pasture rather than tilled in the way their forebears had. But old habits die hard, and that of exceptionally early rises and hearty lunches in a farmhouse kitchen, which could contain the whole of Viv's flat with room to spare, continued. She indicated to turn left off the dual carriageway onto a narrow winding road that climbed up to the base of the rocky outcrop where the monument had been erected. She slowed before breaching the crest of the hill knowing the treat she had in store, a breath-taking view of the sea and the islands in the Forth, the Bass Rock glistening as if in reach. Once a prison for dissenters, and known as Scotland's Alcatraz, the Rock was now a sanctuary to a gannet colony and it shimmered with their guano. Reached by specific tour boats, it was on her to-do list but somehow hadn't happened yet.

Viv's window for doing Suzy and Tom's hair was from 10.30am to 11.15am. However, as she drove up the front drive she was flagged down by Suzy's mum who had obviously been hovering in the garden of the cottage she lived in. 'Any chance you could do me first today?'

Viv checked the clock on her dashboard, knowing that Suzy would have a fit if she wasn't on time, and said, 'Sadly not. Suzy is expecting me and asked me to be prompt so I'm guessing she wants me in and out before doing lunch for the men today.'

'Okay, okay. I'll put my meeting off for as long as I can. But don't be late. I'll still be in a hurry.' Viv was rarely if ever late, and saw this as a sign that Mrs Spencer was stressed out about something that had nothing to do with her hair.

Viv smiled, put the window back up and headed to the main house; lunch for the grooms and farm men was a priority. Calling it a farmhouse was doing it a disservice, since it was a muckle pile of Victorian stone, remodelled in the

1960s with a new façade to make it look Georgian. It had what looked like two symmetrical semi-circular single storey wings on either side but as soon as you went inside the architecture was higgledy-piggledy. Manicured lawns decorated the front but the back of the house was definitely a working farm with barns and stables and horseshit as far as the eye could see. As soon as Viv pulled up Suzy came out of the front door with her hair wrapped in a towel.

'Hello, Viv. I saw my mother nobble you on the way in. Don't worry about her, she's always got some important meeting or other. Come through. We're in here, the men will be in for lunch . . .'

The kitchen was a hub for many things and evidence that cooking was a serious everyday project hung on hooks around the walls and from the ceiling. Whatever Suzy made during the day it was on an industrial scale. Some pots were big enough to boil a baby in. Jugs, Tupperware containers in various sizes, sieves, colanders – every possible culinary tool was available, although nothing small enough to deal with a meal for one like in her own kitchen. The heart-warming smell of half a dozen loaves of bread sitting on a cooling rack at the side of double Belfast sinks permeated the room.

Viv said, 'No worries – I'll be well out of your way before lunch time.' She set up quickly at the far end of the kitchen away from the Aga, since it already had a huge pot simmering on top. She pushed aside an unruly pile of *Farmers Weekly* on a dresser, plugged in her dryer and laid out her tool-roll. Suzy lifted a chair onto Viv's mat and sat in it. Not a minute wasted.

Suzy called out, 'Tom, wash your hair, Viv's here.'

'So what can I do for you?'

'The same as last time. I managed to get it to sit up after using that stuff you recommended.'

'That's good. Does that mean you've not had to go locally since then?'

'Nope. Been able to wash and dry it myself. It's been a godsend. You'd be proud, even when we've been going out to dinner.'

Suzy had spent a fortune and at least an hour and a half daily going to her local salon to have her hair blow-dried. So this was good news indeed, and would make Tom's life much quieter. Suzy wasn't easy to live with when her hair was flat; the fact that she wore a riding hat most days didn't help one bit.

Tom arrived at just the right moment, his cheeks rising like shiny Mackintosh Reds when his face broke into a smile. The tension in the room dissipated and Suzy's shoulders dropped. Tom was one of those men whose presence made everything better. A man whose miraculous good humour was constant. 'Hi, Viv, how lovely to see you. How are you?'

Viv wondered how much of a swan he was. To maintain such good humour was often costly. Was he paddling like fury beneath the surface to keep that smile on his face? If he was she'd never seen a hint of it. She said, 'I'm fine, thanks. You?'

He filled the kettle and in a smooth automatic action placed it on the warming plate of the Aga. 'I'm off to Ireland today, with Suzy's mum. She's judging and I'm going along for the ride.'

Suzy glared at her husband. 'It's not quite your turn yet.'

Tom put a hand up to his lips. Suzy smiled, shook her head and slipped the gown off and handed it to Viv. 'Thank you.' She raised her eyes. 'I'll leave you two to have a proper catch-up.'

Viv thought that for him to go anywhere just for the ride was unlikely but he was such an exemplary son-in-law that maybe she'd misjudged him.

Viv said, 'The forecast isn't bad. Where are you crossing?'

'Stranraer. There's no way we'll get two days without rain it's not called the Emerald Isle for nothing. Just so much rain.' He shrugged and took a seat. Viv wrapped a new gown round his shoulders.

'We can't be far behind them in terms of rainfall.'

'You're right, on the west coast, but across here in the east there's a different climate and we could do with a bit more rain at the moment.'

Viv had noticed on the way in that the two paddocks flanking the drive that ran parallel to the main road weren't their usual lush green. 'I thought the front fields were looking a bit sad.'

'Too heavily grazed. We can usually cordon off a section and move the horses round. But it's been too dry. I mean we often get a dry spell in February but not like this. Must be global warming.'

'Too dry is not a complaint you'd hear in town. Although we had a frost this morning.'

'No. You townies aren't affected by such things as the weather.' He grinned. 'Too busy socialising.'

He was wrong about townies – they were just as obsessed by the weather. She'd noticed how often it had come up in her conversations with Sal. Viv gave it some thought, how often did it influence how her day was planned? The drier the weather the better as far as she was concerned but that was the extent of her concern. 'Shall I just do what we usually do?'

'Yes, please. I never have to think about it from one of your visits to the next so you're doing something right. The barber used to cut it so short I'd have to wear a cap for the first three weeks.' He laughed. His jovial personality wasn't his only side. Anyone who met him would think him a gentle kind of soul, and he was, but in order to keep the family business going on the trajectory that he'd started he had to be savvy and astute. The horsey world was a licence to print money if you got it right and the flash cars out back were testimony to that being the case.

'So, Viv, is life treating you kindly? Got a new man in your life? Can't imagine that you haven't.' He laughed. 'What a catch you'd be.'

This was a frequent line of questioning from clients who were determined to see her married off. Tom asked her the same thing every six weeks and she always gave a similar answer. 'No time for that sort of malarkey. Too busy with this and that. Where about in Ireland are you going to?' Swift change of subject was usually the best course of action.

'Not far from Antrim this time, easy drive. Nice hotel, hearty food and wine.'

'Doesn't sound too shabby but I'm guessing you have pretty good food and wine here.'

He glanced round and lowered his voice. 'Suze is a great cook but recently she's been so busy with the horses that we've been having boil-in-the-bag food.'

Viv laughed. 'No way. They don't even make that any more.'

'You know what I mean though. Just open the packet and stick it in the microwave.'

'I don't believe you. Suzy is a cordon bleu cook and she wouldn't let you eat junk. Besides I bet you're a pretty good cook yourself.'

He nodded. 'I make a mean sandwich. I'll make you one sometime.'

'That would be very nice but today I'm under pressure. Your mother-in-law has a meeting.'

'Oh, she just gets anxious when we have to be somewhere at a specific time. Her meeting is in Ireland and isn't until tomorrow after lunch time but she wants to get on the road.'

Viv finished and lifted up her mat ready to take out to the back door and shake it into a bin.

'I'll take that for you.' Tom took it out of her hands and headed for the back entrance returning with a clean and folded mat. 'Here, let me get your cheque.' He went into a room across the hall, which she knew was his office, and came back brandishing a cheque. 'I've put a little extra on it so that you can buy yourself a drink.'

'Why thank you. I'll raise a glass to you next time I'm out on the town.'

'I'd like to be a fly on the wall to see that.'

For some reason there were clients, and Tom was one, who enjoyed living by proxy and imagined her to be a 'girl-about-town' with a lifestyle that he was missing out on. If only he knew that she'd rather spend hours at home in her PJs than socialise for fifteen minutes.

Suzy's mother was waiting with her hair wet when Viv arrived. This would be another swift session. She said, 'Tom rang. Said to offer you coffee since he forgot.'

Viv shook her head. 'No thank you. I imagine you want to get going as soon as you can.'

'It'll only take me a second to make you a coffee. The kettle has boiled.'

Viv had had industrial strength coffee before heading out to East Lothian but Mrs Spencer was not easily dissuaded from a mission so she let her carry on. Once she sat in the chair the job was simple.

'My blow-dry has to last me a few days.'

'Doesn't it usually?'

She shifted in the chair. 'I suppose it does but I'm meeting some important buyers and want to look my best.'

'Are they buying horses or are you up for sale?'

She laughed. 'Oh you. We have a couple of last year's winners that we'd like to move on. They'll be great at stud.' Her voice quivered.

This was territory that Viv had no clue about but felt an inexplicable wave of sadness that such beautiful animals were commodities. She tried to think of something to say but couldn't. Mrs Spencer had trophies all over the place – testimony to her career as an international judge. Amazing that she'd flown all over the world to give her opinion on a particular breed of pony which she'd rescued from the brink of extinction and which now carried an impressive price tag. Her attitude to horses was definitely not cold so her edginess was anxiety about something else bubbling up and finding the only way it knew to come out. Soothing brush strokes and the heat of the hair dryer soon had Mrs Spencer as calm as she could be. Conversation was impossible without shouting.

As soon as Viv had thrown her kit into the back of the Rav she stretched, shook her arms and legs out and cricked her neck from side to side. She took in a huge breath and let it go really slowly. Her next client deserved a clean slate.

Chapter Two

By the time she arrived back in Edinburgh it was almost 2pm. Her next client had parking which made life easier, but she had to go through the palaver of speaking to an attendant who would allocate her a space, then there was the process of signing into the building and wearing a visitor's pass. She nodded to Bill on the first desk. He was on the phone but winked and pointed to the sign-in sheet. She did as directed then took the lanyard that he handed her, draped it round her neck and headed for the lift. She had to walk between two giant planters with this month's choice of exotic species in them. Beyond those, creating a barrier on either side, were eight-foot high glass screens. She'd already had her scissors out and held them up for Bill to see, otherwise the super high-tech security system that was hidden beneath the planters wouldn't let her through. Now she was permitted to continue through the building.

On the surface Bill might look like any other male receptionist but she hadn't been fooled. No one his age with a sedentary job had abs and biceps like his so she'd hacked their system to see what they were hiding. Their tech was the very latest, just out of testing, Bill was not his real name and his sketchy background looked suspiciously like special forces. Thankfully, now she was through, Bill would already have buzzed to let her client, Robert Burns, know she was on her way up. But as if that wasn't enough, she still had another citadel to breach before she'd get to see him. Stacy, his secretary, who was more bodyguard than woman, answered the telephone on his behalf.

Her formidable presence had protected him for years and she clearly enjoyed the power. She wasn't in the slightest fond of Viv whom she considered beneath her and seemed confused by her boss's attitude to a mere hairdresser. Stacy bristled to perfection as Viv approached her desk.

Viv said, 'Hi, he should be expecting me at,' she glanced at her wrist, '2.15pm.' It was only 2.10pm and Stacy nodded to a bank of comfortable chairs with the day's newspapers on a table at the side. 'I'll let him know you are here.' She didn't make eye contact with Viv but wore her usual look of disdain, which evaporated as soon as she spoke to her boss. Viv wondered about the cost of such wild swings in mood; they surely couldn't be good for her.

Robert stepped out of his office and came over to Viv. He rubbed her arm, took hold of her kit bag and carried it into his inner sanctum. Viv felt Stacy's eyes burning a hole in her back. She couldn't remember having done anything specific to offend the woman but there was obviously some real or imagined transgression.

'I see Stacy's in a good mood today.'

He blurted a huge guffaw. 'That'll be a first. Stacy doesn't do good moods for other women. She's strictly a man's woman, which is odd because she isn't at all a temptress.'

'You mean she's that grumpy with all women?'

'Well, I think she has a special place for you in her wrath, which is probably my fault since I'm obviously fond of you.'

'Well thanks for that. What are we doing today?'

'Same old same old if you don't mind. I've got a meeting in . . .' he glanced at his computer, 'twenty minutes, can we do that?' Whatever Robert did here it was on a minute by minute schedule. Who'd have believed that looking after people's money would be so demanding? What was wrong with a friendly bank manager?

'Take a seat. I'll have you sorted in no time.' She swung a gown around his shoulders and used a water spray to dampen his hair. He was organised and kept a spare shirt at the office, especially for his hair cutting days. Viv knew he couldn't bear tiny shards of hair anywhere down the inside of his shirt and had learned that the only way to avoid an afternoon of scratching was to change once she was finished. The fact that he wasn't in the least shy about doing it while Viv was still around probably added to Stacy's wrath since she wasn't party to such intimacy. As she left she glanced in Stacy's direction but her head was down as she flicked through a fascinating pile of papers on her desk. No love lost but awkward, and all in a day's work.

She parked the car in the Grassmarket and jogged up to the West Bow. She wanted to freshen up and read through a few notes before heading off to her old department at the university.

Chapter Three

The applause subsided. Viv glanced at the woman who had chaired her session.

The acting head of department smiled, 'Well, that was a great response. They enjoy controversial speakers.'

Viv gathered up her notes from the podium and squared their edges against it. She raised her eyes to the woman. 'It was fine. Slightly disappointing that so few women asked questions. Are they all shy or is it to do with the culture in the department?' She slipped her lecture notes into her rucksack wondering which bit of her lecture had been controversial; she thought she'd been tame. She rolled her shoulders, relieved that she hadn't pursued a career in academe.

The woman's back stiffened. 'I'm not sure what you mean. A woman did ask a question.'

'There were twelve or thirteen questions. Only one from a female and it was about my process not about the lecture.'

'Don't you think it's the luck of the draw on the day?'

Viv shrugged. 'It could be. But if the department cultivated confidence in the students they'd have challenged me more. When I was a student here, visiting academics got a pretty tough time from us. We were hungry to know everything. Not just both sides of the argument but everything else; its context. We'd rip stuff apart. I thought this lot were . . .' She stopped. From the corner of her eye she noticed a group gathered by the lecture theatre doors.

'Ah. I'm guessing we do have some who'd like to challenge me. Thank goodness. Come on, let's get a drink in the bar where they'll relax and we'll find out what they really think.'

The woman bristled. 'It would be more than my job's worth to go drinking with students.'

Viv stopped herself from shaking her head and bit the edge of her lip instead. The world is made up of team players with the odd maverick willing to stick a spanner in the works. She knew who she'd rather be with. 'That's fine. I'll let you get back to whatever you need to do. Thank you very much for having me. It was . . . interesting.' Viv stuck out her hand and the woman shook it without enthusiasm.

As Viv reached the door the first question came from a young woman with cornrow plaits and the smoothest, most flawless skin Viv had ever seen.

Viv raised her hand. 'I don't know about you guys but if I don't get something to drink I'll die of dehydration. Come and join me if you like.'

All six of them, three men and three women, nodded their approval and followed her out of the George Square theatre, across the garden and into Teviot. Nothing much had changed since she'd been there as an under-grad. Most of her time as a post-grad had been spent at New College, which was its own little biosphere, without booze on site. Teviot, the social heart of the university, was a different world. The smell of beer and hormones permeated everything from floor to ceiling. It made her smile. The students milling around were as badly dressed as in her time but their efforts to look shabby seemed more self-conscious. Edinburgh prided itself on being a Russell Group university, which meant you had to have straight-As, done a platinum Duke of Edinburgh Award, bred canaries (so that your CV would stand out) and a whole lot of other bells and whistles to get a place. There were continual protests about it being elitist, having too many students from public schools and not nearly enough from the state sector. Ironic, since as soon as students graduated they'd do everything possible to remind people, employers especially, just how elite their university had been.

She approached an area with enough seats for them all to gather and tossed her rucksack onto one of them. 'Okay. What can I get you all?'

They looked confused. The woman with the cornrows said, 'We'll buy you a drink. What would you like?'

Viv hesitated but understood the ethics of buying and sharing food. 'I'll have a half of cider. Organic if they've got it.'

The woman beamed. 'They do now.' The others gave her their orders and she and one of the guys went off to the bar.

Viv took her seat. 'So, you have questions about the lecture?'

A guy wearing a khaki hoodie, jeans and a pair of Converse shoes, said, 'How did you get into Freud from anthropology?'

She grinned. 'Name one department in the university where you wouldn't find Freud.'

One of the women said, 'Well, he's not welcome in psychology.'

'Ah. It was ever thus in the psych department here. "Rats and stats" we used to call it. Only interested in numbers.'

Another said, 'But surely Freud's completely out of date?'

Viv paused a beat. 'I suppose every theory goes in and out of vogue but we all need someone to butt up against, so even if you don't agree with him he's useful as someone to fight with, or use as a sounding board. I was interested in the fact that people either loved or hated him. And by the way, hate is way too big an investment for most things and especially so for a dead person's theories. There was no middle ground with Freud and I think everyone deserves a fair hearing.'

The guy who'd asked the first question cocked his head. 'So were you trying to rescue him?'

'I suppose that's one way of seeing it. I did think he got disproportionately trashed and usually by people who'd invested in him then discovered he was only human. I wanted to show that it was unresourceful to throw the baby out with the bathwater, which is what happens when people are disappointed. They cease to be reasonable. I don't think he was any angel but I kept finding that he was either deified or demonised and neither seemed right. Not many humans are that good or that bad.'

The woman arrived with a tray of drinks and put a glass of cider in front of Viv. 'Hope I haven't missed anything.'

'No. You haven't.'

Khaki top shrugged and took a gulp of what looked like a pint of orange juice. Then said, 'I don't agree. I think more of us need to make a fuss about the things we don't agree with.'

Viv nodded. 'You could be right but it's better to go into a fight armed with the best information you can muster. Apologies for the military analogies.'

Cornrow plaits said, 'I can't understand why, if you're a feminist, you can have anything to do with Freud.'

Viv smiled. It wasn't the first time she'd been called out on this. 'I had psychodynamic psychotherapy. Without Freud that therapy wouldn't have been available. I guess what you're really asking is – what do I think about the whole penis envy thing?'

The woman nodded and shifted forward in her seat. 'Yes. It's too absurd to give it any kind of credit.'

'The standards we expect of great thinkers are unrealistic. He was human. He made mistakes. And if it's not okay for him to make a mistake then we set unrealistic standards for ourselves. We're all fallible. I want to be able to make a mistake and say, "I got that wrong." It shouldn't make me a bad person if there were a ton of other things that I got right. We're too quick to condemn. Don't get me wrong, I'm no Pollyanna. If someone makes mistakes that are cruel or cause lives to be lost . . .'

The woman interrupted, 'I get that but he was not a very nice man.'

'According to whom?'

'I've read loads of stuff that . . .'

Khaki top interrupted. 'That's part of the issue. What we read is always skewed. The author is giving their opinion.' The others all started chatting over one another.

Viv said, 'Exactly. That goes back to my point about people either loving or hating him. When I wrote my book there wasn't much in the way of middle ground.' She drained her glass and checked her phone. 'Look, I have to go but if you have anything else you'd like to ask just fire me an email. I'd be happy to help.' She handed them each a card with her email address on it. 'Thanks for the drink. It totally hit the spot.' She went to the bar and paid for another round to be sent over.

Chapter Four

Outside she checked her phone messages. Jules, who she hadn't heard from in a while, could wait. No one else demanded a reply. She pulled her rucksack onto her shoulders and jogged round the outside of McEwan Hall, over to Forrest Road, then down Candlemaker Row, hoping she'd given them enough to think about.

As she waited to cross the road her phone rang. 'Hi, Ellie. How are you doing?'

'Not bad. I'm just finishing up in the Signet Library and thought you might like to grab a drink.'

Viv smiled. 'Sure. Where? I'm just at the bottom of Candlemaker Row.'

'I'll meet you at Bobby's Bar in five minutes.'

Viv about turned and walked back up the hill toward the pub. Her phone rang again – Ellie? 'Hi, everything okay?' Silence. She glanced at the screen. It was the number that had been calling her and remaining silent. Someone was holding but there was nothing to identify where or who they were. 'Fuck you,' she said calmly and switched her phone to vibrate, then continued up the hill. However many times she'd jogged past this place she hadn't managed to cross the threshold. She pushed the door open and entered a heaving, noisy room. Mostly students, she guessed. She spotted a tiny gap at the far end of the bar and squeezed towards it. If Ellie was looking for a good natter it wasn't going to happen in here, the noise was deafening. The barman was working like mad to meet the demands, two hands barely sufficient. She squeezed back to the door and waited.

Ellie arrived out of breath. Viv shook her head. Ellie poked her head inside the door. 'No way. Let's try Deacon Brodie's.' They linked arms and marched back along George IV Bridge to the Royal Mile. Deacon Brodie's was quieter and they found a seat.

Viv said, 'What are you having?'

Ellie shrugged out of her coat. 'Think I'm in the mood for long and cool. Pint of lager should do the trick.'

Viv shook her head. 'You'll no doubt fill me in on this dramatic change in your drinking habits when I get back.'

Ellie was a cocktails-at-dawn kind of woman. Pints were more Viv's thing. She returned from the bar with two of the same and set them on the table. 'So, what's going on with you?'

Ellie supped what little foam there was from the top of her glass and said, 'I knew you'd get it.'

Viv knitted her brows. 'Get what? That there's something up that you need to run by me? It's not rocket science. I haven't heard from you in a few weeks so you've been up to something.'

'You know my stint in the Hague?'

Viv nodded.

'Well someone believes I did a good enough job when I was there to suggest I become a QC.'

'And are you going to go for it?'

'That's what I've been trying to work out. If I go down the QC route it . . .' She took another swig of her lager. 'Actually, I've already started the process but . . .'

'Come on, spit it out. I bet you don't like that someone has 'suggested' that you do it. You think it's being given a leg up or worse that you'd be cheating.' She shook her head.

Ellie pointed at Viv. 'See, I knew you'd get it straightaway.'

'How personal do the questions get?' Ellie's relationship history was chequered at best.

Ellie looked away. 'Pretty personal. I've cleaned up all my loose ends.'

'Do the loose ends know that they've been cleaned up?' Viv laughed. 'I imagine the people you've "cleaned up" will be as grateful as you to be banished from your life, deleted from all your contacts.'

'Shit, my social media.' Ellie took out her mobile and scrolled deleting accounts as she did. 'As a solicitor advocate I've always had the possibility of changing tack, but thought it was too establishment.' She pushed her thin blond hair off her forehead. 'Weird how at a certain age, whether we want to or not, we become the establishment that we've so keenly fought against.'

'For what it's worth I think it's a great idea. The more women up the ladder the better.'

Ellie smiled. 'Anyway, how are you? How's your mum?'

'I'm ticking along, keeping busy. My mum is remarkably well. You know last year she had a series of UTIs. Mand and I thought she might be losing the plot, but not a bit of it. Since those cleared up she's firing on all cylinders. I wish I knew more about her. Seems strange to have thought I knew her then be told that that was only a fraction of her story. I've asked but she'll not say anything. Old school don't tell. Too frightened to be seen to be boasting. Talking of boasting, I've just given a lecture to my old department. They asked me to speak about my book to their final year students.'

'Good turn out?'

'Yeah. I think the third years also got wind of it. I don't understand why they don't have anything at all on Freud. As I said to them, there isn't a single discipline that he isn't used in. But never mind me, how is your life? Have you settled back into Edinburgh? Maybe that's why you're questioning the QC thing. Maybe you're not ready to be settled anywhere.'

'You could be right. Although I have started the process and it's made me think about what I really want. I don't do sure and steady and that's what I'd be signing up to. Feels like a massive shift and I'm not sure I can live up to it.'

'Nobody dies if you change your mind. You're obviously attracted enough by the idea otherwise you wouldn't even have thought it over. I say go for it and if it doesn't work out you haven't lost anything . . . well maybe a few friends in high places but who cares about that?'

Ellie pushed her hair out of her eyes again and glanced at Viv. 'That makes sense. It may not be the work that I'm worried about.'

Viv gave her time to get to what she needed to say.

Ellie took a long draw of her pint. 'I love my parents . . .'

'But?' Viv raised her eyebrows in a question. Ellie didn't bite. 'You can't bear the idea of looking after them?'

Ellie nodded. 'I feel so bad about it. I look at my mum who's always been so beautifully turned out and see that she has food on her blouse that she hasn't noticed. To be fair it could be her eyesight but it's just the beginning of the slippery slope. They need help but are too proud to let anyone in. It's so painful to watch. I'm family – I should be able to do stuff for them beyond the odd shop.'

'Should is shit. If you're not cut out for it you're not cut out for it. Once they got used to having someone around they'd probably like it. It takes time. I'm so glad my mum moved into the Pound.'

Ellie sniggered. 'You shouldn't call it that. But you are lucky.' She took another long draw of her drink. 'None of us are getting out of here alive. Best be as prepared as poss.'

Viv almost choked on her drink. 'Things must be bad for you to be thinking like that. You need a man.'

Ellie didn't look up from her glass.

'Ah. You've got a new man and that might be a problem.'

'We've only had lunch so far.'

'Who is he married to?'

Ellie blew out a huge sigh. 'What is wrong with me? Why can't I just be normal?'

'Because normal is a myth. You could talk to someone, though. If you keep repeating a pattern that at more than one level doesn't work for you, it would be worth knowing why you keep returning to it.'

'I thought you might psychoanalyse me. Do you know anyone you'd recommend?'

Viv rooted about in her sack and handed over a card. 'Give them a call. I'm sure they'll be able to help.'

Now that they'd got the serious stuff out of the way they could get down to the business of gossip and drinking. It could be a long night.

Chapter Five

Going for a run after a late night and with a hangover wasn't the easiest thing to do but she'd forced herself. Now she adjusted the showerhead and allowed hot water to beat down like tiny needles on her head and shoulders. Her scalp tingled with a new eucalyptus shampoo. No better therapy. Being able to turn on a tap and feel this kind of relief was sheer luxury, an exquisite time for regeneration, for ordering her thoughts, not to mention muscle relief. Reluctantly she turned the water off, stepped out onto the bathmat and wrapped a warm towel round her dripping body and one round her head, relishing the sensation of rough cotton on her skin. How did people survive without a hot towel rail?

She dressed and dried her hair. As she switched her computer on her phone buzzed in the hall. Mac's number showed on the caller ID.

'Hi, Viv, are you busy?'

'Funny you should say that. I'm just about to Google something that's been bugging me.'

'What is it?'

'I was with a client, who shall remain nameless, the other day and I saw on a computer screen an invoice for, get this, eco-static foggers. Have you ever heard of them? Anyway it's been bugging me so I'm checking them out.'

He hesitated. 'Funny you should ask. I'm downstairs can I come up?'

'Sure.' She walked up the hall to open the door for him.'

'God, you're looking well. Going somewhere special.'

'Ha bloody ha.'

He shrugged. 'We've had a memo, supposed to be Top Secret. That's why I didn't want to speak on the phone.'

She interrupted him. 'So Top Secret that you're going to share it with me, your most valued discreet colleague.'

'Do you want to know or not?'

'God, yes.'

'Bear in mind that we receive these warnings weekly. But the memo said that we've to prepare for a high-level biological attack. It's not that we're being intentionally attacked. It's a pathogen or flu type of thing coming from China. Only in the last couple of weeks the level has risen from medium to high. It could turn out to be another SARS thing that doesn't really affect us.'

'Well if that's the case, these eco-static foggers make complete sense. I wonder if they were being ordered as a precaution. According to this site they're designed to completely wipe out pathogens in any room. Even where there's lots of fabric. Blah, blah. I'd better not get my breeks in a twist about it yet. But do you think we should be worried?'

'Nah, not yet.' He laughed. 'But never mind that. I hear you apprehended a suspect this morning.'

She laughed. 'News travels fast. It was weird. I'd been for a run round the Meadows and was on the home straight when I spotted a guy acting suspiciously next to a Range Rover with blacked out windows. He grabbed something off the back seat and ran away. Arse. If he'd walked he'd still be in the wind but he bolted, so I ran after him. There was something vaguely familiar about him. I thought maybe from that job on the west coast. The one with the guys using that amazing kelpie pod for smuggling.'

'You knew you'd seen him before?'

'Yes. Well, I wasn't absolutely sure. I thought I'd seen his photograph on a list in HQ, a who's-who of dodgy characters. It was when we came back from that so-called bonding retreat. He'd had a serious haircut but the thick scar beneath his left eye was the giveaway.'

Mac laughed. 'But how did you see that from a distance?'

'God knows. I'm just nosey. Has its upside as well as its downside.'

'Not much of a downside for us at the NTF, but I didn't just come for that. I wondered if you'd be willing to join me in some new training?'

'Is that a real question?'

'Yeah. I've had a memo.'

'God, memos coming thick and fast this week. You should avoid them at all cost.'

'It said to invite members of staff and consultants that I think would benefit from it. So why wouldn't I think of you? Also, it would mean I'd get to spend time with my favourite colleague.'

She snorted. 'You're so full of BS. What exactly is the training?'

'I'll forward you the email. It even has pictures. You'll love it.'

'You're not selling it. You think I'll only do something because of nice pictures? Better send the link.'

He opened his phone and began scrolling.

'You want coffee or something?'

He raised his eyebrows. 'Or something?'

'You wish . . . but maybe the pics will clinch it. I need a project. I'm spending too many hours online. Not a good idea last night since I'd had a few. God alone knows what trail of damage I left behind. I've also had wall-to-wall hair clients, and Jules has been on my case to give her a piece.'

'What about?'

'Why Edinburgh is no longer the gay capital of Europe. She's obviously scraping the barrel. I'm resisting.'

'Let's grab a coffee later.'

'Sure. When? I'm free tonight, are you?'

She hesitated. 'Yeah, okay. I'm going to visit my mum. I'll ring you later.'

'Excellent! Send her my best wishes.'

He wandered back up the hall and the door clicked closed behind him. No sooner was she on her own, when the phone rang. She checked the caller ID – it was Jules again.

'Hi, Jules, how are you?'

Jules, always short on social graces, said, 'You can get your arse into gear. I've got something I need you to do.'

'I'm fine, thanks for asking. What exactly do you think I can help you with?'

'There's some noise about a group of activists moving stuff in the Irish Sea.' This was good. No mention of the gay capital piece.

'Yes, and what do you think I can help with?'

Jules interrupted. 'You'll know that when you find it. Since you've access to super-surveillance I guessed you'd be able to get your guys to find out the kind of stuff that's being shifted or most likely pilfered.'

'Don't know why you think they're my guys . . .'

'You have your ways otherwise I wouldn't be asking. Go girl, you know you want to.' Jules began coughing and hung up. Viv was used to her bluntness but was still surprised when it popped up.

She shook her head and switched off her phone. Jules was something else. Viv hadn't been patient enough to get in the queue for patience, but Jules hadn't even been in the building. Although with Jules you knew what you were getting and because of that Viv was already feeling pumped. She hadn't done a controversial investigative piece for a while. It would be good to get her teeth into something a bit risky. Jules had only asked her to do it because she knew that Viv had handy contacts at the NTF. Still, an investigation was an investigation. She did a quick Google search to see what the recent gossip on Northern Ireland was. There were lots of articles, since a bridge from the mainland of Scotland to Ireland had been mooted by a government minister. She snorted. He thought building a bridge over an ancient arms dump was a good idea. God, there was no hope for us. She closed down her phone and grabbed her rucksack. Time for a familial visit. As she jogged down through the Grassmarket to where the Rav was parked in King's Stables Road, she thought how odd life was. She'd been spending too much time in the wee small hours digging around online places where she still hoped to find reasons for Sal's behaviour in the US. The prospect of a new project came as a relief. Typical that two should come at once.

Chapter Six

She stamped her feet as she waited for her mother to answer her buzzer. A biting wind was blowing from the east, and the heavy grey sky had lifted so it was much brighter than it had been for her run earlier.

'Em. Hello.' Her mother sounded distracted on the entry phone. The Sheltered Housing unit was supposed to have upped their security but Viv couldn't see any sign of it.

'Who . . . who is it?'

'It's me. Viv.' She could hear voices in the background. TV.

There was a pause before the door clicked to open and she pushed her way into the hall. Plush carpets and anodyne magnolia walls lined the entrance. She glanced around and grimaced at the smell of cooking greens as she bounded up to her mother's apartment on the first floor, praying that the smell wasn't coming from there. The door was ajar so she stepped inside and called out, 'Hi. What d'you think they are cooking down there? It smells like hospital food or something.'

Her mum stepped out from her tiny kitchenette. 'There's a lecture on this afternoon so they're giving us lunch before it starts. It'll be cavolo nero or some such that's flavour of the month.'

Viv smiled. Even in a Sheltered Housing block people were picky about their greens.

The TV was muted. 'You catching up on old movies?' She nodded towards the TV. 'You must have seen them a million times before.'

Her mum raised her eyebrows. 'And what's your point?'

'No point. Just that you must get bored since you know the plot line and the endings.'

'For your information every single film that you or I watch is a propaganda machine.'

It was Viv's turn to raise her eyebrows, but she was intrigued. 'How so?'

'Every time I rewatch a film I see things in it that I missed before. If you used your more than ample brain you'd question everything that comes out of Hollywood, or any film industry for that matter. Ask yourself what the purpose of the film is? Who were they trying to reach? And what were they hoping to convince us of? Don't imagine that it's purely for entertainment. It's always a response to something. Small-p politics is everywhere. Oh, and don't think that it's any better today. Besides, I keep the TV on for news and current affairs.'

This was as much of a moral-high-ground speech as she'd heard from her mum since she'd given her and Amanda a lecture about the politics of tobacco companies and why they shouldn't smoke to fill the coffers of people who were already billionaires, while killing themselves in the process. It had occurred to Viv that movies were made as a backlash to certain events but it was surely too cynical to think that that was the case for all movies. She could think of a dozen rom coms that were benign. 'So what exactly can you tell me about this?' She pointed to the TV.

'Well, it was made just after WW2 to raise morale for returning troops who were coming home to an economy that was completely different to the one they'd left behind. It promotes a life that is a fantasy. Women who'd been in combat or working for the war effort didn't want to go back to wearing pinnies, having shampoo and sets at the salon every week, or being told what to do by their husbands. This promotes exactly that model. It was insidious. It appeals to women's guilt. You know the kind of stuff that promotes biological determinism.'

Viv raised her eyebrows again. She'd never heard her mum use this terminology before. She nodded her approval. 'My anthropology tutor would have loved you.'

'Don't be patronising. We've had enough of that from the men.'

'I didn't mean it to be. I genuinely think he would be impressed.'

'The kettle's on. We don't need affirmation from men. So now that you've had your say, to what do I owe this pleasure? You certainly didn't come to discuss movies.'

Viv took out her telephone, scrolled through then handed it to her mum. 'I wondered if you'd ever seen this guy before?'

Her mum stared at the screen then shook her head. She pinched her fingers on the screen then magnified it, and pointed. 'He on the other hand is trouble.' She handed the phone back to Viv and said, 'Right hand corner. He's slightly blurred but I'm sure that won't faze your tech pals.'

Viv had noticed him but hadn't considered that he'd been connected to the theft from the car. 'You think he was . . .?'

'I've no idea what he was up to but he's a Muldoon. They're an old Edinburgh family who were never, and I mean never, up to any good. If he's in your frame he's there for a reason. You'll have to work it out. Tea?'

'Please. The guy with the scar on his cheek stole a package from a Range Rover and I caught him. He's being questioned at HQ. Do you think he could have been a decoy for something else?'

Her mum laid a tray with tea and biscuits on the table and they sat next to each other on the tiny two-seater sofa. Her mum took the phone and had another look at the screen. She pointed. 'I don't know the one with the scar but he's one of the older sons. Although I can't see the family putting up with him as the head of their enterprises. He was always the black sheep.'

'What kind of stuff are you talking about?'

'You name it. The Muldoons are known for money laundering, drugs, trafficking, importing and exporting anything. Once you're into an illegal network there's nowhere you won't go for the next million.' She handed the phone back to Viv. For anyone else, they were simply looking at a tourist shot of Edinburgh Castle taken from the Grassmarket. She slipped the phone back into her pocket. 'If he was heading up their enterprises he wouldn't be on the streets.'

Her mum said, 'You're right, so what was he doing there?'

Viv sighed. 'Who knows? It's in the hands of the police now. Are you going to lunch downstairs before the lecture?'

Her mum nodded. 'Got to keep the old grey cells tiptop. Besides, the speakers we get have done their research.'

'What is it today?'

Her mum pulled a flyer from down the side of the sofa and opened it up. 'Here. That's this season's list. Use it or lose it; isn't that what we're always being told?'

'I don't think you're in much danger of losing it any time soon. These look great. Surely it isn't that witch of a matron that organises these?'

'Oh, no, she's gone. Got her marching orders. An inspector caught her pushing an old biddy around in the laundry. What a relief. Pam, the new warden, is young and fit and I can't imagine why she'd want to work here but she seems to, and she's got contacts so she organised those.'

Viv glanced at the shelves to the right of her mum and spotted an envelope with the name Dr Fraser on it. 'Is that a typo?' She nodded to the shelves.

'Oh, no, I think it must be for you. Someone slipped it under my door. There's no stamp on it and I'm no doctor.'

'How long have you had it?'

'It was there this morning when I got back from the laundry room.'

Viv stretched above her mum's head, retrieved the envelope and pocketed it.

'You not going to open it?'

She sighed, 'Okay.' She took it out, prised it open and removed a single sheet of paper from inside. Same type-written script as on the front read, 'Back Off.' 'Not giving much away are they?' She handed it to her mum who took the corner of it between the tips of two fingers. She turned it over and then handed it back.

'Seems like a lot of trouble to go to, to say so little.' She grinned at Viv. 'The message was in leaving the envelope here in the first place. What they're saying is we know where your family live and we know how to get to you and them. There's CCTV downstairs. We can take a look.'

'You think the warden will just let us see it?'

Her mum nodded. 'She's not at all like the last one. I think someone must have told her about me. She's a bit in awe.' Her mum smiled. 'A little bit late for anyone to think of me as . . .'

'As what mum? A Cold War spy?'

Her mum blew out a breath and brushed away Viv's words. 'You and your fantasy, it'll get you into bother.'

Viv shook her head. Her mother was definitely old school and wouldn't admit to anything she'd done since she'd signed the Official Secrets Act. Viv had gathered snippets. Enough to piece together a life that hadn't been what, as children, she and her sister Amanda, were led to believe. Their mum's 'secretarial work' had involved travelling on different passports to foreign countries or being trained in spy craft (another snippet gleaned from Ruddy and a few forays behind the firewalls of the civil service's online records). She'd called in a few favours but it was worth it. It was difficult to look at her mum now, and believe she'd been fearlessly on the Glienicke Bridge at a time when a selfie would have landed her in an East German gulag. She glanced at the envelope and the flimsy piece of paper and snorted. 'They think this is intimidation? They obviously don't know the Frasers.'

Her mum said, 'That man in the photograph is ruthless. Even the family thought he was a bad one.'

'How do you even know them?'

'There were a few families that your dad was worried about in Edinburgh. The Muldoons were one of those families. He didn't bring his work home often but he said they'd do anything to make a buck. He was angry that they weren't being stopped. In the early days it was easier to trace their ill-gotten gains but now paper money is no longer such a big part of the equation. Still someone else must be onto them. Surely your cyber guys could trace their movements?'

'Since when did they become my cyber guys? I'm the one they call in when they want something done beneath the radar.'

'Talking of radar, let's go and see if we can find anything on the CCTV.'

Her mum locked her front door and they took the stairs to the ground floor where the warden's office was tucked away at the end of a corridor. The smell of cooking cabbage was even more overwhelming than before.

'I don't know how you can stand it.'

'Stand what?'

'The stench of cooking.'

Her mum smiled. 'You forget I am the generation who remembers when there wasn't anything fresh to cook. Everything came in a tin. That smell is a luxury to me.'

Viv snorted, 'Oh, God. I'd die if . . .'

Her mum shot a look over her shoulder, 'Spare me the attitude. The tinned food revolution could happen again, and all you'll have is the memory of that wonderful fresh cavolo nero being lightly steamed on our behalf.'

Viv walked behind her mum with her eyebrows raised. It was entertaining to hear her firing on all cylinders. Whatever she had had for breakfast Viv wished she'd had some as well.

Chapter Seven

Her mum rapped on the warden's door. It opened a fraction with the pressure, enough to reveal the warden sprawled over the desk, papers strewn across it and on the floor, and her phone knocked off its stand. Viv's mum immediately checked for a pulse and nodded, so Viv rang 999. She bent to look at the papers on the floor but her mum said, 'Best not touch anything.'

She gave her mum an I-know-what-the-form-is look then took photographs of the room from all angles. A print on the wall behind the desk was squint. Had there been a proper scuffle? It didn't take long before they heard the sound of a siren approaching. Viv wondered if Sheltered Housing had priority for 999 calls or if it was just a slack day in A&E. The warden was being carted off on a stretcher to the ambulance just as two police constables arrived.

One said to Viv's mum, 'Is anything missing?'

She replied, 'I've no idea. We came to see the warden about something and found her and those papers exactly as they are. We haven't touched anything.'

'Do you know if there's any money kept here?'

'I think she has a petty cash box but I shouldn't think there's much worth stealing.' The female police constable used a pen from the desk to hook the handles of the desk drawers. In the bottom one she found a cash box, still locked. 'Doesn't look as if they wanted cash.'

Viv stood to the side with her arms crossed. Her mum was a natural.

The WPC said, 'I noticed a camera on my way in. We'll check it out.'

Viv said, 'We were hoping to get a look at something from earlier.'

The PC raised her eyebrows, 'And why would you want to do that?'

Her mum interrupted, 'Oh, we just had a delivery and wanted to see who the messenger was.'

'I'm sure there's some data protection rule that would prevent just anyone looking at the footage.'

Viv pulled out her NTF lanyard and held it up. 'Will this do?'

The PC nodded and started looking for the recording on the warden's desktop.

Viv said, 'Since IT is my thing I can probably locate that footage quite quickly.'

The PC reluctantly stepped aside. Viv's phone rang. It was Mac. 'Are you still with your mum? There's a report coming in of an assault on the warden at her sheltered accommodation.'

'Wow, how come that would find its way to your desk?'

'I'm watching the police ticker tape.'

Viv shook her head. No idea why he would do that. 'We're in the office now, just about to check the CCTV.'

'That's convenient. How badly hurt was the warden?'

'Don't know. She's gone off in an ambulance. There are a couple of PCs here. Do you want to speak to one of them?'

She handed her phone to the WPC. 'It's my boss from the NTF.'

The woman listened then handed the phone back to Viv. 'He said if we needed anything enhanced he'd fast track it. Handy knowing people in high places.'

They gathered round the desktop and stared at the screen. As ever, the footage was slightly blurry but it was clear enough to see that whoever had been in the office had known where the cameras were and had sprayed them with hairspray to obscure the image of him. But they did catch a good view of his hand before he covered the first one. He was bold enough, with only a baseball cap pulled down over his eyes and his jacket zipped up over his chin. He must have brought the spray on purpose.

Viv stood by her mum who said, 'The only evidence we have on him is that he entered the building, which in itself isn't a crime.'

The WPC said, 'Yes, but spraying the camera is. He wasn't wearing gloves so his prints will be on the office door or elsewhere. Nice clear shot of his hand there too. Right, we'll close up here and go and see if anyone has anything to tell us about this.'

Viv pointed to the frame on the screen. 'There's no blood so what did he use to knock her out? Did he punch her or hit her with something he brought for the purpose or from the office? The hairspray suggests his visit was premeditated.'

The WPC gestured to the door, so Viv and her mum went into the corridor and the two PCs walked off to the entrance hall.

Viv said, 'Could have used the hairspray to knock her out? It wasn't a big can.'

Her mum raised her eyebrows. 'It's not difficult to knock someone out. Even now I could take you out with one move.'

Viv snorted, 'Yeah, sure.'

Her mum took a step towards her, 'I'd hate to kill you just to prove a point, but one of these days when you least expect it maybe I will.' Her mum grinned.

'One of these days I'll find out exactly who and what you are.'

Her mum winked. 'Don't go holding your breath.'

'It isn't a pissing competition, mum. I'd genuinely like to know.'

'Right now I think it's best if we concentrate on speaking to Mrs Cheng Jung.'

Viv looked confused. 'Why?'

'Because in the shot before he sprayed the lens, I caught her image, at the edge of the screen. She must have let him in. Let's go and see if she's back. She's a woman of habit. Goes to the shop at the bottom of the lane at the same time every morning.' Her mum looked at her watch. 'She's usually back by now.'

'So do you track everyone's movement just for fun?'

'Not everyone. Not many of them are able to get out, but the ones who do mostly have routines that they don't change, so if they did we'd know something was up. It's not called sheltered housing for nothing you know.'

Viv followed her mum upstairs but instead of turning right to her own flat they went left. Three doors along on the left side of the corridor her mum knocked and waited. There was no sound from inside so she knocked again.

Silently the door opened and Mrs Cheng Jung immediately blurted out, 'I didn't mean to let him in – he barged past me.'

Viv's mum said, 'No one is blaming you. I just wondered if you noticed anything about him. Was he carrying anything in his hand? Was he checking behind him? How tall was he compared to you?'

'Yes, he did check behind him. I think maybe there was someone outside. I didn't see anyone standing around but they could have been inside a car. When he pushed past me his elbow was almost at my shoulder. I am only five feet one inch.' She pointed above her head. 'He was pretty tall. Maybe six feet. He smelled of smoke.'

Viv's mum smiled. 'That's great. Thanks for your help.'

Mrs Cheng Jung had the door closed before she'd finished her sentence.

Viv said, 'Are we going outside to pick up any new fag butts?'

Her mum nodded. 'Why not? People do tend to discard their fag ends before entering a building these days. But I'm wondering, if someone would do this to get your attention, what else would they do? The note is one way but they might have tried to get something from the warden and she didn't comply.'

Viv smiled. 'Don't you think you're just excited to be doing something other than watching old movies on TV?'

'Maybe. But I've also not got much time before lunch and the lecture this afternoon.' She shot Viv a cheeky grin. 'Busy life, you know.'

Viv shook her head. 'I've got a meeting with my new solicitor later, but I'll fill Mac in on what we've discovered. Not sure why he would get involved but he'll know who to pass it on to.'

'How is Mac?'

'Great. He sends his best wishes.'

Her mum's face lit up. 'He's a good man.'

'I know he is.' An awkward silence fell. 'I'll get going and see if there are any butts near the door.'

'I'll come out with you. There's no point in you taking them away.'

So they went to scour round the front door and over by the car park. There were lots of butts but only one that looked fresh and hadn't been crushed. Viv handed her mum a small evidence bag.

'So this is the kind of thing you carry around in your pockets?'

Viv pulled out a pair of latex gloves and pulled one on. 'I'll get that.' She picked up the cigarette end and dropped it into the small poly bag that her mum was holding open. 'Team work! You can give this to the PC.'

In a rare gesture of intimacy her mum rubbed Viv's upper arm and nodded to a small Fiat in the car park. 'What do you think?'

'It's cute. Why?'

'It's mine.'

Viv glanced at her mum and back to the car. 'I don't understand. You've never . . .'

'Oh, I've always had a licence but never drove when your dad was around, and never had a need for a car of my own.'

'Didn't you have to resit a test because of your age?'

She tapped the side of her nose. 'Apparently I've not lost my touch.'

Her mum was a master at evading questions. 'So you can just get in that car and go anywhere you like?'

Her mum grinned and nodded. 'Not that I plan on going anywhere beyond the supermarket. But at least I don't have to stand and wait for buses on a wet, windy day.'

Viv scratched her head. 'It didn't occur to me that you waited for buses. I thought you had your groceries delivered.'

'Vivian, there's more to my life than waking, eating and sleeping you know.'

'Oh, I get that. But a car for God's sake.'

'It's second hand. But runs like a wee dream.'

In all of Viv's life she had never seen her mum behind the wheel of any car other than a dodgem. It was too much of a stretch to imagine her scooting about Edinburgh and not doing anyone damage. She shook her head. 'I'd better get going. Not sure I can cope with any more surprises.' She walked across to the Fiat and checked out the inside. It was cute. Grey leather upholstery piped with cream. It was the kind of car she imagined being driven by a student whose daddy had insisted she have wheels while she was away from home. You could squeeze two in the back but they'd have to fold themselves in and keep their knees up to their chins. She glanced back at her mum, who was still standing at the door, arms crossed, and grinning like the Cheshire cat.

She called over to her. 'Cosy. Probably not chauffeuring the Scottish first eleven.'

Her mum shrugged. 'Don't bet on it.'

Viv threw her a wave and headed over to the Rav, jumped in and started up. Whatever next? This was not the first time she'd had to give herself a talking-to about ageism, but she couldn't get a vision of her mum behind the wheel with her nose almost touching the windscreen out of her head. She reminded herself what she did know about her mum and conceded that she'd probably driven in more dangerous situations than she had. Get over it. She's a veritable Pandora's box and no doubt there'll be more surprises when she chooses to let them out.

Chapter Eight

Her first client was in Inverleith. But she had a quick call to make first on her new solicitor, a woman who'd been highly recommended by an old university friend. On the way to York Place her phone rang, the third time in the last couple of days where she didn't recognise the number. Again no one spoke when she answered but they didn't immediately hang up – some nut job looking for a way to ease his boredom. She slid her phone back into her pocket and poked around the central well for change for the ticket machine. She thought about the other calls. They usually came when she was about to leave the car. She glanced around. The street was busy with vehicles and pedestrians, an easy place to blend in. She got a ticket, stuck it on the windscreen inside then pressed the fob to lock the car. She didn't expect the meeting to take long but she hoped she could see the car from inside the office.

The receptionist asked her to take a seat but Viv preferred to pace and keep an eye on the street. If she craned her neck she could see the Rav. She checked out the boards with properties for sale, and was shocked at how high the prices were. She was here to make sure that the assets she'd been left by Sal were put into a trust the same way as Dawn's had been. She didn't want anything to do with them but had to find ways of making sure that neither woman would go unrecognised. In Dawn's name a scholarship had been set up at the Conservatoire in Glasgow but it was still too early to tie up Sal's assets. What if it had all been a huge misunderstanding and she came home?

As long as she could eat, sleep and have shelter she wasn't big on acquisitions. Sal had known that, but she'd also known that Viv would act wisely in a crisis. Once called into the actual office of Helena McFergus, she felt as if she were in good hands. The woman spoke in a matter-of-fact manner and the meeting only took half an hour. Ms McFergus had done her prep and all the paperwork was in order, so it was a simple case of signatures and clarity. Viv had already set out her initial ideas and McFergus had understood exactly what she needed.

When the solicitor said, 'That's everything for now,' Viv rubbed her face with relief and glanced out of the window. She spotted a man loitering on the opposite side of the road. Dressed from head to toe in black and wearing shades was a bit of a give-away, so he wasn't the sharpest knife in the drawer, or maybe he didn't care whether she saw him or not, a more worrying scenario. In the few minutes it took to say goodbye and reach the street he was gone. As she approached the Rav she had a strange tingling feeling at the top of her spine. She glanced over her shoulder and scanned the other side of the road. Nothing untoward. Even so, she knelt on the ground and checked beneath the car. Nothing. Now she was paranoid.

Chapter Nine

By the time she pulled up at Arboretum Place she'd made a couple of calls. She got out of the Rav and wiped her hands down her thighs. This visit was usually a quick in and out but even so she always looked forward to seeing Diana and what she was working on. A partner in a criminal law firm, she had seen some low-life in her time but was the coolest person in a crisis that Viv knew. She rang the bell and waited. The door swung open and Diana mouthed a silent hello. Her hair was already wet but she had her mobile pinned to her ear. She beckoned Viv into her vast kitchen full of every gadget to make life easier, and pointed to the kettle. Viv shook her head and began the familiar process of setting up her work area. Large tarp on the floor, dryer plugged in, scissors, combs and brushes out, and lastly she swirled a gown round the back of a chair. Diana's shoulders were up round her ears as she listened to whoever was on the other end of the line. Her eyes occasionally reached for the sky and she shrugged to Viv that she couldn't do anything about the situation. Viv leaned against the worktop and flicked through a day-old newspaper. When Royals were on the front page you knew there wasn't much happening in the world or there was and leaders were doing everything possible to keep it hidden. Finally the call was over.

'Oh my God, I'm so sorry about that. I said I'd call him back but he's one of those guys that won't take no for an answer and I . . . never mind. Can I get you anything?'

'No thanks, I'm fine. Let's just get your hair started.'

To the rest of the world Diana had the thickest hair imaginable but she had two large tell-tale circles of waxy skin at the back where hair hadn't grown for a few years. Cutting it didn't take all that long but drying it still did.

The chair faced a plate glass window that looked onto a large manicured garden at the back of the house. Leaves had been swept and plants looked as if they would spring into life the second Diana gave them permission. Viv thought of Sal's garden at Doune, which was tidyish but not controlled to within an inch of its life. If she hadn't spent time out and about with Mollie she probably wouldn't have noticed the garden one way or another. Now she could see that nothing would grow in Diana's garden without her say so. It was weed free.

'You want me to do what I usually do or are you up for a change?'

'Same as last time please. It worked really well and it stayed in shape. Even this morning it looked good.'

Viv sectioned off the back, exposing the patches of alopecia before trimming the baseline. 'You do realise that hair is organic. Like carrots or potatoes you can never do exactly the same twice.'

Diana said, 'Fair enough. As close as you can get though.'

Viv continued taking sections and cutting. 'I know you don't speak about clients but have you heard of a family called the Muldoons?'

Diana's shoulders tensed. 'Anyone involved in the law in Edinburgh has heard of the Muldoons. Why do you ask?'

'Just wondered.'

'You're not the type to idly just wonder. But if I were you I'd do everything possible to avoid them. There's nothing good will come of a connection with them.'

'I hear they have fingers in all sorts of pies.'

'You heard right but they're not any kind of fingers or pies that you'd want to touch. Be careful, Viv. I'm not kidding when I say they are bad news.'

'Are they violent?'

'They are clever. They never used to be as clever as they are now. They do make people disappear. I'd hate to lose you. Who would look after my hair?'

Viv could tell she was trying to make light of the conversation so she changed tack. 'You working on something tricky then? That call sounded as if you couldn't get a word in.'

Diana, a consummate pro, said, 'Nothing that I can't handle. I should have delegated but I said I'd speak to him later in the day. I didn't expect him to ring back when I was washing my hair. I couldn't exactly tell him that.'

Viv laughed. 'I've had some people use the most fabulous excuses when I've been doing their hair.'

'I bet you could write a book about the stuff you see in our homes.'

This was a frequent concern, sometimes a test. 'There's no way I'd tell the things that I see. No one would let me do their hair, if I did. It's like being a lawyer. Client hairdresser confidentiality's part of the deal.'

'I suppose . . . Old man Muldoon died last year and there's been a family feud. Two brothers vying for the top job. The one that's most likely to step up is ruthless and a bit more careless than his brother. Also the sons, although they have degrees, are almost as power hungry as their father. I was approached a few years back to defend them but didn't take the case. Colleagues, friends have had "accidents" when the Muldoons didn't get what they wanted. They are definitely best avoided. Am I being clear enough?'

'Surely someone has to bring them to heel?'

Diana's eyes almost popped out of her head. 'I mean it, Viv, don't even think about it.'

'Okay. I'll do everything I can to avoid them.' This wasn't possible now, since they'd already goaded her into action, but best keep that to herself. What was it that made the powers of these family dynasties so long lasting? Her mum knew that her dad had thought they were a bad lot. Had that been a clue as to why they now had her in their sights? 'Can I show you a photograph?'

'Sure.'

Viv took out her phone and found the photograph. She handed it over.

Diana nodded. 'Yes, that's the one you least want to cross.'

'Okay, thanks.' So her mum was on the money.

Chapter Ten

As soon as she finished up with Diana she called her mum. The phone rang and rang then went to answering machine. It seemed that her mum's social life was more active than her own. She didn't leave a message; she'd try again later. She drove to her next client, in Cramond, through one of Edinburgh's toughest neighbourhoods. Pilton was a known drug dealer run and suffered from all the social deprivation that went with that: food and health poverty, debt and the consequent violence that accompanies those things. Fifty yards beyond this, with only a railway bridge dividing them, was one of Edinburgh's wealthiest areas. Davidson's Mains, a short corridor that led into Barnton and Cramond, acted as a buffer zone, a kind of no man's land. With each step you could add another couple of zeros to the family income. Cramond was leafy, the space surrounding the houses a sure sign of affluence. She pulled into the drive of her next clients, a husband and wife team who'd long been retired but had always worked from home. Inheritance had been a handy cushion for them, but they couldn't stand to own that they'd retired or didn't need to work. Sandy came out to meet her and insisted on carrying her kit in. He was beginning to stoop but wasn't the type to give in to ageing. He'd dabbled in antiques and always wore a cravat and corduroys, the uniform of his trade. His wife Sara had been a picture restorer and they were both hippies at heart. The house, stuffed with antiques and memorabilia, or what most people would see as clutter, made it difficult for Viv to find a space to put out her kit. Sandy took her bag straight up to their bedroom on the first floor. The window was wide open and a cold wind howled in. The view was spectacular. Their large wrap-around garden backed onto one of Edinburgh's most prestigious golf courses, not too shabby and not overlooked by anyone.

Sandy rushed over and pulled the sash down. 'I forgot about that. Sara'll have my guts for garters. I'll go and find a heater. He left and Viv moved a couple of small armchairs to one side and set up in front of a full-length mirror on a mahogany stand. Sara came in balancing a tray with a flask of coffee and some homemade buns on it. She squeezed it onto a dressing table; perfume bottles and jewellery clattered to the side as she made space for it.

Sara shuddered. 'It's freezing in here. I bet he's had the window open all morning.'

Viv smiled and accepted the mug of black coffee that Sara handed to her. She wrapped her hands round it, relishing the warmth.

Sara held up a lock of her hair. 'Oh boy, do I need your help. I'm tempted to have the whole lot shaved off.'

Viv had heard this many times before. 'I expect you wouldn't much like the result. But by the time we're done here you'll not be so frustrated.'

Sara flopped into a chair and Viv swirled a gown round her shoulders. 'Shall I?'

Sara sipped her coffee and nodded. 'Yes. Do your thing. It's always a miracle to me that you can transform this burst mattress into something respectable.' In reality a five minute blow-dry would tame her locks but she'd have to want to do it. Sara had other priorities and despite her years looked like a Pre-Raphaelite model.

Sandy arrived with a fan heater and plugged it in. 'There. That'll make a difference.'

Sara said, 'You'll probably blow a fuse. You know that old wiring can't take any extra load.'

'Oh ye of little faith. It'll be fine, I unplugged the computer and the TV just in case.'

Even if they had the funds they wouldn't upgrade the electrics, or, God forbid, downsize. It was their home and they were like a comfy pair of slippers residing in it. No matter that it was a cavernous place built for a wealthy merchant who'd have had staff to look after his every need, including laying and stoking coal fires all day. They had crammed it with the things they loved – art, antiques, and his impressive collection of military memorabilia that must take hours of dusting to keep it pristine. Once finished with Sara she did look tamed, no longer a vision of chaos and eccentricity. Sandy was much more self-conscious about his hair. Old boy's parting and waves controlled with whatever he'd bought from Mr Trumper's website, he had hair that tested Viv's barbering skills to the limit, and by the end her fingers ached with the use of tapering scissors. She was delighted, if amazed, every time they made their next appointment, aware that their hair was probably one of the last luxuries they'd let slip.

On her way to the car she noticed a sapling growing out of a chimney and a dark mossy watermark where a rhone had overflowed down the wall. Perhaps Sandy wasn't able to keep up with jobs that required a ladder and was putting them off – sad, and no way round it, since they were too proud to accept help.

Chapter Eleven

She stopped at Mo's mini-market to pick up essentials on the way up the Grassmarket. Even at this time of year and on a cold windy day she had to duck and dive to avoid tourists snapping photographs and taking selfies beneath the bulk of the Castle's rock. No such thing as 'out-of-season' any more. In the flat there was a message from Mac on her machine saying he'd see her at Bella's at 7pm. That left her a couple of hours to do some research.

Time flew when she was poking around in places she shouldn't, so it was almost 7pm before she looked at the time. 'Shit!' She grabbed her rucksack and headed out.

She called to Mac who was just getting out of his car opposite Bella's. 'Hi there, good to see you, hope you're as hungry as I am. Smell that deliciousness.'

He grinned. 'That's what I like about you. You're either full on or off. Not much middle-ground when it comes to sensory perception.'

'Oh, I don't know, I think I've got some very sensitive middle ground. I just don't have occasion to show it around you.'

'What's that supposed to mean?'

She shook her head. 'No idea why I even said that. But who cares – my belly's rumbling. Let's get inside.'

He held the door and she skipped in below his arm catching a light smell of lemon from him. 'Nice. What's that you're wearing?'

'God knows. Whatever came to hand in the shower.'

She shook her head. 'I don't believe that. You would never just buy any old smelly.'

They sat at a table by the window and checked out the specials board before Bella arrived with menus.

'How are you guys?' She pointed to the board. 'Just in time. There are only two portions of the . . .' She didn't finish the sentence.

Mac said, 'We'll have them.'

Viv nodded. 'Yes, done.'

Bella said, 'Wine?'

Mac said, 'Half of house red,' looking at Viv for agreement.

She nodded again. 'And if there's any sourdough.'

Bella grinned. 'You two are so predictable. I'll get the bread.'

Viv said, 'So what's this training you were on about and who else is going?'

'So far I've only asked you but I've got another couple in mind.'

'What are we supposed to be training for?'

'I'm guessing the Boss had a memo from on high and he's prodding us to get our fitness up to speed. You won't have too many problems since you run and swim regularly but some of the others in the unit are total couch potatoes. Could barely run a bath.'

'I'd put money on there being more to it than improving our fitness. I've had a request from Jules who might not be the most sensitive editor but she's always good at catching the rumbles. She wants me to check out some activity on the west coast.'

'Nah. I genuinely think the Boss has got it in the neck from above and he's booked us space at Camp 16 to keep them happy.'

'We'll see.'

Bella arrived with a basket of bread and a dish of butter. 'Don't eat it all or it'll put you off your mains.'

'You must be kidding – I'm starving.'

Bella and Mac both shook their heads, but Mac said, 'We don't know the meaning of the word starving but she's definitely on the wrong side of blood sugar.'

Meanwhile Viv was already munching a slice of sourdough and groaning with pleasure. 'I'll have to clear time in my diary. Although I'm due time off, I wasn't imagining holidaying at Camp 16. I've a wee notion to sign up for a dig.'

'What, archaeology, down on your knees for days at a time kind of dig?'

She agreed through a mouthful of bread. 'Sure. I have to find a way to disconnect from tech and I've read there's a call for volunteers. It's not until April, so there's a while to think about it yet.'

'You're nuts. I'd be sure to check the long range weather forecast before you sign up for anything. You could think of Camp 16 as archaeology of the physique. Digging out your strengths and weaknesses.'

Bella approached with two steaming shallow bowls of cassoulet. 'Here you are. Enjoy.'

There was nothing to beat Bella's dish of the day and for the next few minutes they were silent and appreciative.

Mac spoke first. 'You think Jules really does have an ear to the ground?'

Viv nodded. 'She's got a magpie brain. Then she homes in on her target and transforms into a terrier. Gotta respect her for her ability to keep worrying at a loose thread. I did scout around for outlier stories about Northern Ireland but there's nothing much beyond . . .'

Mac interrupted her. 'The stupid bridge. There's never been a more stupid idea. Well, certainly its proposed site.' He pointed his fork at her. 'I don't think anyone who applies to be a politician should get to be one. Only people dragged kicking and screaming to the job should get to do it.'

'Agreed. Anyway, as I was saying, there wasn't anything that struck me, but she must have something in mind. She said I could get 'my' boys to help me. Bloody nerve since . . .'

'She could be right though. You don't spend eight or nine hours a day listening to chatter for nothing. I'll run it by them. See if anyone's heard anything worth following up.'

Viv was about to speak when a woman came to the table and loomed over them. Viv leaned back and Mac did the same. 'Oh, hi.' He pushed his chair back and stood up. 'How are you doing?'

The woman said, 'I'm fine. I'm guessing this is the famous Viv Fraser?'

Mac flushed. 'Viv, this is Caroline Pettigrew.'

Viv went to stand up but the woman said, 'Don't get up on my behalf.' Her tone told Viv as much as she needed to know about what she thought of her. Mac flashed Viv an apologetic glance. The woman caught him. 'Don't worry, I'm not here to cause a fuss. I just guessed from your email replies that there was someone else, so I did a bit of digging and the name that kept coming up was Viv Fraser. Your photographs don't do you justice.'

This was clearly not meant as a compliment but Viv didn't rise, although it took all she was worth not to.

'Nice to see you, Mac.' She nodded and walked back to a table on the other side of the bistro where another woman sat staring into her coffee.

Viv looked at Mac and immediately felt sorry for him. 'Nice friends you've got, DCI Marconi. Were you ever going to share that wee gem with me?'

'I met her at a conference. There was a group of us – she obviously took my friendliness for something else.'

He was squirming, so she smiled and said, 'Easily done. Got a couple of tee shirts myself to prove it.' They continued eating but the momentum had shifted. 'She got something on you?'

His head jerked up from his food. 'No, she has not, but she's one of those complicated women who has got better men than me into bother, and I want nothing to do with her and made that clear in my email responses. She's not the type to be easily brushed off.'

'She's a charmer. Can't understand why you'd resist her.'

He sighed. 'I should have known not to engage with her at all. But I was in a group – we were meant to be doing an exercise.' He shook his head. 'Honestly, I didn't do anything to encourage her.'

'You don't have to justify your actions to me. You're an adult, she's an adult.' She shrugged. 'So far, so fair.'

'You're kidding, right? She's unhinged. The first time I heard her laughing I knew she was deranged. It was completely disproportionate to what had happened. The laugh was an attention-seeking thing.' He cringed. 'I hate that.'

'Now, now. Hate is way too big an investment.'

'No, I mean it, it makes my skin crawl.'

'What's her job?'

'She's an inspector in Border Control. I outrank her but she's dangerous.'

'Only if you don't outwit her. Come on, Mac. She'll soon move on to someone else.'

'You think? The conference was last year and she's emailed me almost weekly since then.' He took out his phone, scrolled through and handed it to her. 'We're now into triple figures.'

Viv glanced through a couple of the emails. 'For fuck's sake, that's harassment.' She pushed her chair back and stalked off towards the table where the two women were settling their bill. Without any preamble she said, 'One more email and I'll file a harassment charge on his behalf. He's too polite, too much of a gentleman. Me, not so much. And with what he's got on that phone already, you'd be looking at stacking shelves somewhere.'

The woman opened her mouth to answer but Viv walked away from the table and went to the loo. By the time she got back to Mac the women were shuffling out the door.

'What did you say to her?'

'Do you really want to know?'

'I can fight my own battles.'

'I know you can, but sometimes a woman's touch is what's needed.' She grinned. 'Pudding?'

He rubbed his hands over his face. 'Christ, I'm sorry about that.'

'I'm not seeing any sign that it was your fault.'

'Okay, let's share a tiramisu.'

'Done.' She nodded to Bella who was drying glasses at the counter. 'Any tiramisu left?'

'Always got some somewhere. One or two?'

Mac stretched then rubbed his hands over his washboard belly and said, 'Just one. The cassoulet was delicious and I've only got a tiny space left.'

Great recovery if you didn't know him. Viv gently put her hand over the top of his as he started to play with the cruet set. 'Oy, that's my job. She'll not bother you again.'

'I wouldn't be too sure about that.'

'Imagine if you had sent a woman hundreds of emails hassling her for dates using language like that. Your arse would be well and truly in a sling. There's no way you'd still have your job. Why should she? If she knows what's good for her she'll take heed.'

'The phone messages were even worse but I've deleted those.'

'You do know that nothing is ever completely deleted? So if you needed to retrieve them I could do that in a heartbeat.'

He glared at her. 'For God sake, I didn't come up the . . . I have my own way to deal with the situation thank you. I'll keep you posted. By the way, are you doing anything on Sunday?'

'Depends on who's asking. If it's you I can probably fit you in.'

He spooned up a piece of tiramisu and stared at it suspended before him. 'My mum asked me to ask you if you'd like to come for lunch sometime. I said you'd be busy but I thought I'd better run it by you.'

Viv's eyes came out on stalks. 'Why would your mum ask me to lunch? She hasn't seen me since I was about sixteen and I wasn't the type to impress her then, so why now?'

'If I'm honest it's probably my sisters. They keep hearing about you and are curious so I'm guessing they've badgered her into inviting you. Honestly, it's no biggy. I'll just make your excuses.'

'Like hell you will. I'd love to come and meet them all again. Will your dad be there?'

He raised his eyebrows. 'Of course. He won't say much since he's never learned to get a word in with four women about the place, but I'm sure he'll give you a reassuring nod now and then. But are you sure?'

She grinned and nodded. 'Can't wait. Your mum is an even better cook than Bella if your efforts are anything to judge by.'

He shook his head. 'You've no idea what you're letting yourself in for.'

'It'll be fun.'

He leaned back in his chair again. 'Remember there's no such thing as a free lunch.'

'What? Do you think there's an ulterior motive?'

He shrugged. 'Just sayin'.'

Chapter Twelve

Viv Fraser woke up to the sound of a ticking clock. It wasn't in reach so she pulled back the duvet and swung her legs over the edge of the bed. She shuddered when her feet hit the cold linoleum floor but padded over to the windowsill and tapped her hand on the top of the alarm clock. Three minutes before it was due to go off. Through a slit in the curtain she could see the first signs of a sunrise. She stretched. There hadn't been much sun over the past week. Camp 16 was as comfortable as anyone might expect a special forces training camp to be, with gruelling early morning starts and classes late into the night. It was the kind of place where if you couldn't stand the heat etc etc, so the numbers quickly dwindled. She understood that whether you were in or out could be decided if you had one bad day. Whatever the weather they had trained hard. The whole point was endurance.

The female instructor was nothing like anyone she'd ever met. Super-fit obviously, skin like warm Galaxy chocolate, but a voice that could persuade the ice caps to melt. Confusing though, since she displayed empathy and special forces were not known for that. This was new.

Viv was used to Scottish weather, but consecutive days of rain, mist and low cloud had certainly dampened her spirit. Seeing a hint of sunshine put a spring in her step. The mirrors in the shower block were already running with condensation and the floor was awash. Her ablutions didn't take long, since she couldn't stand the smell of institutional soap. It was regarded as soft to bring one's preferred bathroom products. She slipped into her fatigues then made her way along the corridor and down to the refectory on the ground floor. The room was buzzing with chatter and the sound of crockery being stacked. She went into the galley, filled a mug of coffee and grabbed the last bacon roll from the hot plate. She glanced at her watch and frowned. She was late. How had that happened? No time to socialise. She gulped the coffee and chewed on her roll as she made her way to the quad where she'd be given instructions about the day's expedition. The enclosed walls of the quadrangle had been darkened by coal smoke and moss grew around the base of windows and downpipes. With tall Victorian buildings on four sides, and only one high arch which led to the drive and fields on the other side there was no way the sun could dry off the persistent dampness peculiar to the west coast of Scotland. Viv had been to the camp before, but over the past week had become more familiar with its layout and the rhythm of the day.

They had been worked hard and her muscles complained less than they had in the first days. Now if she was asked to drop to the floor and give fifty press-ups she could do it. In fact she was beginning to enjoy it. Mac, on the other hand, was not. He had pulled a muscle in his shoulder during the first week and everything he did was painful. He was no slacker and foolish enough to push through his own pain threshold. The instructor allowed him to continue since if they'd been on real manoeuvres he would have had to keep going anyway.

She glanced around to see if he had arrived. He hadn't been in the refectory and it was not like him to oversleep. Then she spotted him on the other side of the quad speaking to Ruddy, their boss from Edinburgh, and the person who had insisted that they take this course.

Ruddy beckoned her over. 'Hey, Viv. How are you holding up? I hear Marconi's been having a tough time.' He grinned.

'I'm doing fine. No longer feeling as if my limbs are on fire, so something's changed.'

'I have a job for you.'

'But we're not through here yet.'

'I think they'll survive without you. Follow me.'

Mac glanced at her and shrugged as they marched across to a door that led into an area where Viv assumed admin happened. They went downstairs and along a corridor where domestic staff would have once scuttled about preparing meals and performing the tasks that a big country house required. Ruddy led them to what could only be described as a situation room. Instead of maps on the walls there were large screens with satellite photographs covering an area on the west coast. During the last week she had seen countryside, been up hill and down dale, scaled rock faces and waded through rivers in spate. So now anything indoors seemed like a picnic. Someone in the room adjusted the focus, and the map on the screen became more detailed. She could see buildings tucked beneath the cliff on the shoreline in Argyll.

Ruddy said, 'You're both familiar with this place. Remember canoeing round the headland?' He pointed to the screen, outlining a peninsula where both Viv and Mac had been on a team-building weekend when a drug operation had been discovered.

'When are we going?'

'As soon as you can get your things together. The Land Rover will be waiting to take you.' He pointed at the screen again. 'You'll remember there was a set of caves? Well, it seems as if those are back in use. Probably not by the same drug ring but someone else homing in on that territory. They sound more sophisticated than the last lot and most of their operations are at night, which means they have good marine and satellite communication. We are guessing that they also have weapons and access to serious money. We've set up an information-gathering unit in the retreat centre that you stayed in. So far, whoever they are, they haven't been worried by our vans moving in and out with equipment since we've used hydro-electric as our cover. You both know what the land is like, so make sure you take what you'll need from the storeroom. You'll get dry-suits when you arrive there. You also know what the temperature of the sea was like in June and July. In February you could die within minutes without a suit. There is one bonus – fewer midges, but I'd take a midge net nonetheless.' He grinned. 'I don't envy you this one. We think they could have Middle Eastern backing and are a lot less worried about using arms than us Brits. Mac, you'll head the team. Viv will look after IT and you'll have access to four other men, actually three men and another woman, all of whom have trained here at Camp 16, so they know their way around night exercises if you need them. It goes without saying that I don't want to lose anyone on this assignment, but the activity off the coast has escalated. They, whoever they are, obviously have something specific and high-value they're bringing in. Now, take that Land Rover at the archway.'

Viv and Mac both nodded and headed back to their sleeping quarters. The military were pretty draconian on gender issues, so men and women were still segregated as if men didn't have sex with men and women didn't have sex with women. Mac pointed the way to the storeroom. It was like a supermarket, but filled with military paraphernalia. Ruddy hadn't said how long they'd be away, so she took extra long-johns and socks and shivered at the thought of getting into a dry-suit at all. What could be worse than squeezing into a suit that was already damp? She prayed for a drying room, but last time there had been power outages so there were no guarantees even of consistent electricity. Maybe that's what the hydro-electric cover was about. Just maybe the hydro company were putting in a better supply. On second thoughts if the military were going to use the retreat for training purposes and missions like the one they were about to go on they'd have to up their game as far as tech was concerned. First time around the retreat had prided itself on the absence of IT. It must have vastly improved otherwise they wouldn't want her there at all. Fingers crossed that everything had been upgraded.

The Land Rover idled at the other side of the archway. She threw her bags into the back and was about to climb in when the driver said, 'Actually, one of you guys is driving. The others are already there.'

Viv jumped out and went round to the driver's door. 'Okay, I'm fine with that.'

Mac arrived and put his things into the back. 'How come you're driving?'

'Early bird and all that. Besides you'll be able to rest that shoulder while you navigate. I don't know if I'll remember exactly where to turn off. Remember how the track was washed away in that storm? D'you think they'll have put in a proper road?'

He shrugged. 'I imagine since the MOD have taken it over completely all will be tickety-boo. You can be sure everything will be in working order and we'll even have super-fast broadband.'

She smiled. 'I was wondering about that. Last time the WiFi was poor to non-existent. There's not much I can do without it.'

'I'd lay bets that all of that has been sorted, otherwise they'd not send us.'

Chapter Thirteen

They drove off down the long drive, closed in by mono-plantations on either side, until they reached the main road. The temptation to turn left and go home to see Mollie and sleep in a comfy bed was strong but she took a right in the direction of the coast. A low wintry sun seeped through the trees onto the loch opposite. The journey ahead should take less than an hour, which would mean they'd arrive in plenty of time for lunch.

Mac settled into his seat. 'I've been hoping I'd get to lead a team up here again. Rough terrain exercise is a whole other world to working out in the gym.'

'You don't have to remind me of that. I remember running along the beach and through knee-high heather. After the last couple of weeks we should be more than prepared for anything. How did you get on with the canoeing expedition?'

Mac replied, 'I thought my fingers would fall off and I'd never walk again I was so cold. I'd do it all again though just for the satisfaction of thawing out at the end of a day catching bad guys.'

'D'you think it's in your blood?'

'No. I think I'm compelled to be a good guy.'

She snorted and glanced over at him in the passenger seat. 'You think? Why did you choose to do this? I mean you could have been a tip-top corporate lawyer, or a hedge fund manager or some other geezer who made money from making money for other people. Why this?'

'I don't know really. I couldn't stand to be in an office all day surrounded by traders. I might have enjoyed family law but I'm not really motivated by cash. I'm motivated when I see the smile on someone's face when we put someone who has hurt them or their family behind bars. Not much to beat that. I like to think I'm making a difference to people's safety. What about you? Why are you here? You could be swanning around the New Town in Edinburgh cutting rich people's hair, going to cocktail parties.'

She laughed. 'You're kidding me, right? I hate cocktail parties. I'd rather stick hot needles in my eyes.'

'One of these days I'm going to hold you to that. I am. I'm going to get some of those famous hot needles and make you choose.'

'Good luck with that! But seriously. We both have to be a bit mad to prefer doing this kind of stuff to sitting with our feet up watching the footie.'

He laughed. 'I love sitting watching the footie. Wild horses wouldn't drag me from a good game except of course a decent crime to solve. That's why we're so well suited.'

This was the second time in the last few months he'd said that. She knew it was a test so she turned to him. 'I think you're right, we are well suited.'

He straightened in his seat. 'You don't mean that.'

'Yes, I do. We work really well together, we, well I, like the food you cook.'

She slammed on the brake as a stag leapt out of the forest onto the road and raced to the other side. 'Shit.'

'Whoa! Well read. I didn't see it.'

'I saw those branches moving before it appeared.' She blew out a breath. 'If we'd hit it, it would have totally caved in the front of this contraption.' She checked the rear view mirror, luckily nothing behind them, and continued. 'That's the first time in my driving career that I've had to do a proper emergency stop. Thank God for anal driving instructors.'

He shook his head. 'Did you have your coffee this morning?'

'I'm not sure I'd call it coffee but I had something wet that was supposed to be. Whatever it was still fired up my adrenals. But if you need more caffeine we could stop in Oban and stock up. There won't be many goodies where we're going. What do we need?'

'We'll not starve.'

'Last time we had vegan food and no caffeine. I had the jitters on the first day. It'll only take us five minutes to stop and get real coffee and a supply of chocolate.'

'Honestly, Viv, you're supposed to have grown out of chocolate addiction by the time you're thirty.'

'That's bullshit. Haribo maybe, but definitely not chocolate.' She grinned at him. 'Five minutes tops.'

'Okay. We might as well fill up with fuel. Better safe than sorry.'

'What are you expecting? We've only to keep an eye out and report back. He didn't say anything about intervention.'

Mac raised his eyebrows. 'You'll get the hang of it one of these days. When you're told to help yourself to the store cupboard it's a sign. What exactly did you pack?'

'Wouldn't you like to know?'

He laughed. 'For God's sake, Viv, it isn't a competition. I've got to keep you safe but it would be good if you were also prepared.'

'There's no way either of us can do that. I've got my trusty Gerber but hopefully I won't need anything beyond WiFi.'

They pulled into the first petrol station on the edge of Oban and filled up. While Mac covered the petrol Viv answered a call. It was another silent one. She hadn't had her phone on much while at Camp 16 and this could be the first time in days she'd had a signal. She slid the phone into her pocket and shook her head.

Mac climbed back in., 'Something up?'

'Nah, just some nut job who rings me every now and then but doesn't speak.'

Mac raised his eyebrows. 'We should have the number checked out.'

She shrugged. 'It's weird. They only seem to ring me when I stop the car. Like now. It's almost as if they can see me. I wonder if they've put some kind of tracking on my phone?'

'That would mean they're more sophisticated than your average nut job. We'll get it checked when we get back to Fettes.'

She grinned. 'You are so sweetly naïve. And no offence, but d'you think I can't do something like that in a tenth of the time it would take Fettes' cyber guys?'

He shook his head. 'I don't want to know.'

Serious amounts of coffee and chocolate were purchased. Who knew when there might be an apocalypse. Viv liked to be prepared. They drove south out of Oban. This part of Scotland was incredibly beautiful but the roads wound in and out like a fiddler's elbow and, with blind summits every few hundred metres, it was like being on a waltzer. Mac was a good passenger.

Eventually they reached a longish straight. She said, 'We must be getting close. I recognise this bit.'

'Yeah, it's just there. Oh look, tarmac! I bet we're in for military precision all round.'

'Did you know about it?'

'I'd heard rumblings after our last visit that it was an ideal venue for training but hadn't heard that it was acquired.' He rubbed his hands together. 'We can grumble all we like about cuts in the police force but when we do joint ventures, I mean when the military get involved, there's such an abundance of efficiency it makes my heart feel all warm.'

They turned off the main road and drove for at least another mile on smooth but single-track road. 'Why d'you think they've kept it single-track?'

'They won't want to make it easy for people to have access in or out. Not that that will stop the nosey parkers. If people want to see what's down here nothing will stop them. Scotland's right of access and all that.'

'They could put up MOD signs.'

He laughed, 'If you had any idea how much land the MOD has in Scotland you'd be horrified. But they don't want the public to know that. Although locals don't take long to work out who their neighbours are.'

She dropped down the gears and began the steep descent to the retreat house.

Chapter Fourteen

As they drew to a halt a man with an undeniably military bearing came out to meet them. Dressed from head to toe in black he stuck out his hand to shake Viv's. 'Connor O'Malley. I believe you know the house?'

Mac nodded and also shook hands with him. 'I see there have been a few changes.' He gestured to a brand new building tucked in against the lee of the hill. 'That wasn't here the last time. It was more of an open sided lean-to for equipment.'

O'Malley replied, 'Yes. It wasn't secure enough for our needs but it is now.'

Viv raised her eyebrows. 'Are canoes and life jackets in much danger here?'

O'Malley laughed. 'We've upgraded. Once I've shown you your room I'll give you a tour.'

He took them inside and another man, also dressed in black, went out to the Land Rover for their things.

O'Malley showed them to a room on the first floor with two single beds and its own bathroom. Viv looked at Mac. 'Where's your room?'

O'Malley said, 'Oh. We thought . . .'

Mac said, 'Whatever you've heard, we'll need separate accommodation.'

O'Malley scratched his head. 'That could be difficult.'

'Don't make me pull rank. Just show me where you sleep.'

Viv smiled and slipped inside her room. Mac and O'Malley took off down the corridor. The windows had been triple glazed. The place was warm and didn't look as if it had been used much since its upgrade. A faint smell of paint hung in the air. She sat on the bed and bounced. The mattress was also an improvement on the last one. There was a tap at the door. She opened it.

'Hi.'

The man who'd gone out for their bags stood laden with all their kit. 'You want to take what belongs to you?'

She grabbed her bags and pulled them inside. 'Thanks. You didn't need to do that.'

'An order's an order, Ma'am.'

She bristled. 'I'm not anyone's Ma'am.'

'Okay, Ma'am.'

She shook her head and closed the door. The military functioned with a clear hierarchy. She wouldn't be the first person to try to puncture it and fail. After checking out the loo she went back downstairs.

Mac was already waiting. 'I've drawn the short straw on accommodation. They're still redecorating at the other end. My room has plastic on the floor and tins of paint lying around. O'Malley has given me a blow-up mattress.'

'You could sleep in my room since it's only for a couple of nights.'

'What makes you think that? This kind of surveillance could take weeks.'

'No way. I've got hair to cut. One week tops and I'm out of here.' She stepped closer to him. 'You already smell of paint. You can't sleep there. Would you share with one of the other guys?'

'No. They're below my rank. It wouldn't work.'

'Does that mean we're equals?'

'It means that I'm the head of a team that you are a consultant with. Equality is a shape-shifter.'

'What's that supposed to mean? Come on, let's get a look at what needs to be so protected.'

They stepped outside and O'Malley was waiting for them. 'This way.'

He pressed a fob as they approached the new building. An alarm sounded on the door. It clicked open and they stepped into a cavernous shed.

'Wow!' An eight-seater RIB sat on a trailer at the far end, with double doors that probably opened directly onto the shore. Canoes and all sorts of water-sports kit were hanging in neat rows against the back wall. A new concrete floor made the space look much bigger than the old shed, but the footprint couldn't have changed that much. An industrial-sized boiler with a myriad of pipes sat in one corner.

Viv said, 'Ground source heat pump?'

O'Malley nodded. 'State of the art. Bore-hole on the shore.' He pointed to the double doors. 'It's just out there to the left of the slip-way.'

'That's new. We had to drag our canoes up the rocky beach after our weekend of survival. Good improvements. They could make us soft. The house is definitely warmer than it was last time and that was at the height of summer.'

O'Malley smirked and pointed at the canoes. 'We only use the canoes if we need silence. The RIB gets into places most other craft don't. As for the heating, it's a godsend. The drying facilities are now second to none. We've also got state-of-the-art tech which should make your job easier.'

'Any idea what my job is meant to be?'

'We've been monitoring activity on the other side of the peninsula. It's on the increase and their movement is always at night. Got to be suspicious.'

'Not to mention stupid or maybe just brazen. I mean, whoever they are must know that the coastline is monitored.'

'Not necessarily. If they are foreign they might assume that our maritime police function in the same way as their own. Which could mean policing of an entirely different sort, where they're being paid under the table for it.'

She said, 'I think most countries are watching their boundaries more carefully than ever. Have we got satellite images on a live stream?'

O'Malley nodded. 'Yes, Ma'am. Come, I'll show you the office. It's quite different to the old one.'

They followed him back toward the house, but instead of going in the front door they skirted round to the side. A benign-looking wooden door opened into a porch with rows of coat hooks and a bench where outdoor clothes could be removed and hung up. Then O'Malley used his fingerprint to open another door.

'Wow! Isn't this slightly OTT for the west coast of Scotland?'

He grinned. 'It's called future proofing. You'd think it was OTT but it is amazing what we're picking up. People don't yet think of the sea as the biggest highway on the planet. We still imagine people move around by plane or train or lorry, but the shipping lanes are more crowded than ever before with legal and illegal traffic.'

The room was set out just like the control room at Camp 16 – huge screens with live feeds of movement from small sailing craft to huge containers right out into the Atlantic.

Viv rubbed her hands together. 'When do we start?'

Mac said, 'Child in a sweetie shop moment, eh Viv?'

'Beats the tech I've had to cram into my cubbyhole at home. Although we've yet to see what it'll let me do. Ruddy wants me here for my unorthodox methods. The military setup will have firewalls within firewalls.' She grinned. 'Not a problem to by-pass if you all leave me to it.'

O'Malley said, 'We've had orders to let you loose.'

She rubbed Mac's back. 'Music to my ears.'

He shook his head. 'You still have to answer to me. So don't go keeping stuff to yourself.'

She said, 'I'm peckish.'

Mac said to O'Malley, 'See that? Classic avoidance tactic. But since she hasn't started yet and I'm also hungry, let's head back to the house.'

The smell of cooking wafted through from the kitchen. They took seats on the bench in the refectory and someone brought out a tray of piping hot bowls of soup then laid out crusty bread with a selection of meats and cheeses. Mac smiled. 'This is a far cry from the vegan meals we had last time we were here. Things are looking up.'

Viv raised her eyebrows. 'You can say that again. I don't know how we managed to survive the last time.'

O'Malley nodded. 'We did think about keeping the vegan menu, but when it looked as if the new catering staff would mutiny we decided against.'

'Good call.'

O'Malley said, 'So what's your plan?'

Viv tested her first spoonful but it was still too hot. 'I'll spend some time with those screens this afternoon and see if I can detect any patterns. I'd also like to find out if there have been any land purchases in the area recently.'

Mac raised a finger. 'Actually I heard that in the last year someone sold one of the islands in the Inner Hebrides. I don't know if it was as far south as this but worth checking.'

'I'll get onto that. But I suppose it's also worth us doing a recce of those caves.'

O'Malley looked at Viv. 'Will you want the RIB?'

Mac said, 'I think we'll go overland. We need the exercise.'

Viv faked incredulity. 'I've had enough exercise to last me a lifetime, but if you say so.'

The three of them were tucking in heartily when the door opened and a woman in what seemed to be the standard black uniform came in and saluted O'Malley. She turned to look out of the window and continued past the refectory table into the kitchen. Viv thought that her avoidance of eye contact was surely telling.

She nodded at the kitchen door. 'Is she on your team?'

O'Malley nodded. 'Amber. She was SBS. She's tougher than the rest of us. Don't understand why she's joined us but it'll no doubt come out sometime.'

Viv said, 'I was hoping that we wouldn't need tough. That whatever is going on, we'll discover it online and hand over to you guys or whoever else deals with maritime crime.'

O'Malley gestured with his head where the woman had gone. 'She is also pretty good with tech.'

'Good to know.' Lots of people were good with tech these days but there was good then there was a whole other world of knowing.

Mac stood up. 'I'm going to get organised. We might as well make a start.'

Viv nodded and slurped down the remains of a glass of water. 'See you outside.'

She took the stairs to her room and organised her pack. Why would that woman come and work with such a small group? Special Boat Service was the crème de la crème, maybe something had gone wrong. Working with the

NTF would definitely be a step down. As O'Malley said it would come out eventually. She made a mental note to find out more but now she made sure she had what she needed for a serious hike.

Chapter Fifteen

They could walk to the caves and back in a few hours depending on how the weather behaved. She stared out of the window at a grey foreboding sky reflecting on the sea. It was dull but at least it wasn't raining or blowing a hoolie, yet. A final loo stop and she was ready to go. Mac was waiting at the door. He swung his heavy pack onto his back.

'What the hell have you got in there?'

'Be prepared.' He grinned.

'I am but I'm at least a few kilos lighter than you. Are you planning something that I don't know about?'

He winked. She smiled and pushed him. 'Don't you wink at me, matey. I'd like to know what I'm letting myself in for.'

'I packed a couple of bivvies.'

She screwed up her eyes. 'Why would you? We can easily get there and back in what's left of the day if we get a bend on.'

They began to walk up the track to meet the brow of the hill, where they turned right along the top to join the moorland. Once they were onto the moor it was knee-deep in heather roots, and large areas of bog meant it was slow, tough going.

Mac said after a good half-hour slog, 'You can see why I thought bringing a couple of bivvies was a good idea. The last time we were here was in summer and the ground was bone dry.'

'I still remember it being a rough trek over this stuff.' She kicked a clod of peaty reeds and they splashed right up the front of her legs. 'That didn't happen last time.'

'So how are you doing, Viv?'

'Oh God, is that a question from a boss to an employee or is it my friend concerned about my welfare?'

'You're such a cynic. I am genuinely wondering how you're coping. I mean, there's been a lot to take in and a lot for you to do.'

'Yes, there has been, but I've had help. Not least from your good self. I know that you try to keep me occupied to keep me sane. It works, but the nights are long and she is not ever going to be there again . . . Thank God for Mollie.'

'How is Moll doing with Brian's new training?'

'He's chuffed with her. She seems to love working. But as soon as she comes back to me she reverts to couch potato. Amazing that she can be so enthusiastic about rounding up sheep one minute and curled up by me the next. There's a good deal we could learn from our canine companions.'

'You are already like that.'

'What do you mean?'

'You're like a chameleon. You can become whatever you need to be in any situation.'

'You think? That's not how I see myself. I think I'm pretty consistent.'

He turned back and raised his eyebrows, 'Consistent you are not. I was thinking more like Anansi.'

'And is that a bad thing?'

'In this job you need to be adaptable so being a chameleon is great. But I guess it's pretty exhausting. Is it not?'

'I don't think about it, I just do what it takes to . . . I was going to say please people but I don't think it is always that. There are different ways to have our needs met. Sometimes you can do it without ruffling too many feathers, other times . . .'

Mac said, 'Other times you ruffle people enough to have them take a pot shot at you.'

'That's pretty rare. I mean I did stick a screwdriver into his thigh, if it was the gamekeeper you were thinking of?'

'He's not the only one, though.'

'Well let's not go there. How are you doing? How's the débâcle with Fiona?'

'Luckily for me she has a new love interest. So for now I'm off the hook.' He sighed. 'Some days I'm sorry that the wee one turned out not to be mine. It made me imagine a life that I didn't have.'

'What, you've never thought about settling down and having kids?'

'Not really, not seriously.'

'But it has crossed your mind?'

'Yes, but only fleetingly. Probably not any more than it would cross yours.'

'You've no idea what goes on in my mind. I'll have you know I have a very colourful imagination.'

He snorted. 'I've no doubt.'

'What's that supposed to mean?'

'No one would ever accuse you of being dull, Viv. I don't know anyone who has a more colourful life than you. I mean you cut hair, you write, you snoop.' He dodged the play punch that she threw at his arm. 'I knew that would get you. But honestly, your life is as varied as it could be, although knowing you I can imagine you throwing kids into the mix.'

They had covered quite a bit of ground and she stopped to take off her scarf and unzip her jacket.

'This conversation too hot for you?' He jumped ahead onto a boulder. 'I can see the sea from up here. We've still got a serious march ahead.'

She joined him on the rock and looked back at where they'd come from. 'Still, we've come a good couple of miles. I don't know why we didn't take up the offer of the RIB.'

'There's nothing like a good long walk to get to know what's going on with someone.'

'You got what you were looking for?'

'I wasn't looking for anything in particular.'

She laughed. 'Walking, a long car journey, joining a sewing bee are all like having psychoanalysis. No eye contact means it's easier to let go. Freud was no slacker.'

He shook his head. 'That's what I mean about you being a chameleon. I don't know anyone else who could mention sewing bee and psychoanalysis in the same sentence.'

She laughed again. 'You should get out more.'

They continued chatting while puffing and panting over the rough terrain until eventually they reached a stretch of machair, spongy short mossy grass, full of the seeds of tiny wild flowers, that ran to the top edge of the cliff.

'What a relief to get across that.' She slung her thumb in the direction of the rough heather and bog that they'd traversed.

Mac nodded. 'You're not wrong. My thighs are burning. But think of the exercise.'

'I don't know why you keep going on about exercise. Anybody would think we were a couple of slouchers the way you go on. The last week at Camp 16 has knocked me into shape big time. My clients won't recognise me when I get back.'

Mac walked on then suddenly stopped. 'Smell that?'

She drew in a breath. 'You mean the sea air?' Then she caught it. 'No, you mean the smell of burning.'

He was tall enough to be able to see into an indentation ahead. 'Over here.' He started off and there it was, a dark smouldering area up ahead. 'At least we know that someone has been here before us today. And not that long ago.'

Viv knelt down next to a charred area about two metres in circumference and touched it. 'It's still quite hot. But the centre is wet. It's been deliberately doused. Not just left to burn out. Look there's something on that edge. Let me try and salvage it.' She leaned over the edge of the blackened grass and retrieved a shard of what appeared to be a flap of cardboard box. 'You think this was walkers on the cliff having a barbie and then moving on?'

Mac shrugged. 'Hard to say. But it's a helluva big barbie. Let's see what you've got.'

She handed him the small piece of card. 'Not much to go on.'

He glanced at her. 'These characters along the side don't necessarily mean anything. It could have been a box of noodles from the Chinese takeaway in Oban.'

'You think?' She hunkered back down and poked around the remains of the fire. 'Ah, but this would be unnecessary for noodles alone.' She held up a length of black industrial-strength bale plastic, the sort used to hold packaging together.

Mac said, 'Still doesn't give us much to go on.' He walked to the edge of the cliff. 'But that might.' He pointed.

She joined him and stared over the rocks. Where the rocks petered out onto shingle lay a large length of the same plastic. 'Whatever that was wrapping, it wasn't chow mein.' They both scuttled down the rocks and over the shingle.

Mac lifted it. 'This could have come in on the tide.'

She nodded. 'It could have. But what are the chances of having some of it on the fire and the exact same thing left on the beach? Let's get a look inside the cave.'

Viv was tentative at first. The last time she'd been in this particular cave they'd found one of the tutors from the retreat centre unconscious. The entrance was low and slimy with seaweed-covered rock pools. Once inside it opened up and although it was difficult to stand up straight at least they didn't have to crawl.

'Ah, check this out.' She pulled a large piece of damp cardboard trapped in a fissure in the rock. 'Look familiar?'

It had similar characters written on one side. 'Okay. So that does appear to be a very large carton of chow mein.'

She laughed. 'You. I'll stick them both in my sack and we can take them back to base. The font for characters might be identifiable. We wouldn't be doing our job if we returned empty handed.'

'Whatever's been happening here it wasn't much of a picnic. It looks more like a whole load of packaging was being burned. But why? They could have chucked it in the sea and let the ocean do its stuff. Weird or what?'

'I agree it is weird. They might just have been cold or pyromaniacal. But that's a large chunk of cardboard so the rest of it must have made up a serious bit of kit. No one would carry that over land. So they've brought it in by boat. Curious, but not much to go on and one fire doesn't make a crime.'

They crouched on the floor scouring for any other traces that might give them clues. But there wasn't anything. Not a single fag butt or gum wrapper to be seen. How come that large slice of cardboard had been missed?

They went back to the beach area but light was fading and they decided to call it a day. The scramble back up the cliff proved more of a challenge in the gloaming but they made it with only a few scrapes. Viv stared out to the horizon and saw nothing but a calm grey sea with no activity. Whoever had been here earlier was nowhere to be seen either over land or out to sea. But that wasn't unusual since the west coast wasn't short of places to hide yourself, if that was what you needed, but it was rare not to see any shipping activity or pleasure cruisers or their wakes.

Viv brushed sandy gravel off her trousers and said, 'I think this was a complete waste of time. How long do you reckon it will take us to get back?'

'Not as long as it took us to get here, but I think you're right. It was probably a waste of time. Here.' Mac handed her a head-torch. 'You should wear this.'

'Should is shit!'

He scowled at her. 'What are you on about?'

She adjusted the elastic and put it over her forehead. 'Shoulds, oughts and musts are super-ego led and any time you hear yourself using them it's good to ask whose voice is in your head. Most of the time they are duty words rather than an, 'I'd-like-to-do-this, words'. I had this same conversation with Ellie recently. What is it with you guys and duty?'

'Now who should get out more? I'll have you know that I think duty is a very good thing, otherwise I wouldn't have joined the force.'

She laughed. 'But for whom did you join the force? Who did you think you were pleasing by becoming a man in uniform?' She linked her arm with his. 'It's good to question our motivation for doing stuff. And it's helpful to know if the decisions we're making are resourceful or if we're going to resent them.'

'Right. When you're done with the psychobabble I think we should stick to the cliff-top path for as long as we can. It's used more so will be easier to see.'

'You're the boss.'

He turned and stared at her. 'Got a better idea?'

'How could I possibly have a better idea than a genius like you?'

He took off and she followed. It was tough going in half light. Her head-torch took a bit more adjusting and at first all she could see was Mac's back. A couple of times she came perilously close to the edge without realising. Once the torch was in the right position, and she stayed far enough back to scan the ground in front, they got into a steady rhythm and marched back to towards the centre. It was good to see the warm glow from its lights on the horizon. The land looked deceptively level but there were peaks and troughs in there.

'No one would ever think that there was serious military activity and surveillance going on in that benign looking wee house.'

'I think that's the point. They won't be incognito for long and they'll have to move on, but at least the centre will have had the benefit of military infrastructure. Remember the last time? Not only did the road collapse but the WiFi was non-existent and the generator had to be used 'cause the electricity went down. I doubt that would happen now.'

Just as Viv was about to reply all the lights in the house and the boat shed went out in unison. 'I wouldn't be so sure. Look.'

Mac said, 'Quick, switch your torch off.' And he did the same.

They stood in complete darkness for a few seconds before he whispered, 'A power outage without inclement weather is a no-no. And I don't expect someone has tripped a fuse otherwise the boat shed wouldn't be affected.'

'So, what are you saying?'

'I'm saying I think someone has deliberately cut them off.'

Heavy cloud cover meant that they could see light pollution in the distance but it was of no help to them. A few seconds later the power flickered back on.

'So, what was that about?'

'No idea. But it shouldn't happen. They've got super-backup.' Mac frowned.

'I wonder if someone was testing something?'

'What? You mean someone from the centre or someone outside testing whether they could take their power down?'

'It could be either. No point in speculating until we get back and speak to O'Malley.'

'Odd though.'

'Let's keep moving. We'll find out soon enough.' She turned her head-torch back on and followed Mac.

A lit stove in the room where they'd eaten lunch was a welcoming sight. As they dumped their rucksacks O'Malley came out of the kitchen.

'We've been hacked. Someone managed to interrupt our power.'

'You want me to take a look to see if they've planted something in your system?'

'You could do. Amber's already out there.'

Mac said, 'I think it's worth Viv taking a look. She knows how hackers go off-piste.'

O'Malley nodded. 'Sure, let's go. You coming, Mac?'

'Yeah, I'll tag along.'

Viv shot him a look. 'You could organise some food for us. I'm guessing this'll not take too long.'

'No. I'll come and see if I can learn anything from what you do.'

'Okay. Let's see what the baddies have been up to.'

O'Malley said, 'Find anything out there at the cave?'

Mac shook his head. 'Nada. Total waste of time. There had been a bonfire but nothing to suggest anything illegal's been going on. Viv brought a piece of cardboard back just in case we need to trace it, but we'd be scraping the barrel.'

O'Malley shrugged. 'One less thing for me to worry about then.'

When they arrived in the control room Amber had her head down and was typing at one of the consoles. She quickly shut down the page she was on and the screen went black. Was it Viv's imagination or did she look worried?

O'Malley said, 'Can you let Viv in to . . .'

She pushed her chair back and said, 'I'll leave it to the expert then.' Not even an attempt at disguising her derision and still no eye contact.

Viv took the seat still warm from the woman's presence. As a hacker she had to convince herself that she was a warrior going where others were too scared to venture for the greater good. Otherwise she'd have to put up with the fact that she was a grubby trespasser rooting about in people's metaphorical dirty laundry. Mac and O'Malley chatted above her head as her fingers danced over the keys. Had they noticed Amber's attitude or was she hypersensitive?

After a few minutes she rolled the seat back and said, 'I can't see much. I'll need more time. But I'd like some food first.'

Chapter Sixteen

They finished up their food and each of them went their separate ways. Viv went back to the control centre where she took an adjustable seat and rolled it to the same desk she'd been at earlier. She took the odd note longhand, reassured by having info at her actual fingertips. Amber had wanted to shut down whatever she'd been viewing but Viv found a way back in. A few minutes later Viv was sniggering to herself. The only site she'd found of any interest was *The Leprechaun Lotto*. Looked like Amber had an issue with gambling, although on further inspection her account was totally in the black with a few thousand points to spare. Did points convert to pounds? Viv had no idea but it didn't seem that *The Leprechaun Lotto* posed much of a national threat. There was however evidence of a backdoor breach. Someone had got through first level security. Mucked about a bit with what they'd found but had got no further. They hadn't stayed on long enough to leave a tracking code so whatever it was had failed. Maybe that's why the lights had only been off for a very short time. She traced the attempt back to a local console and imagined some fourteen-year-old sitting in their bedroom warding off boredom by hacking into systems that were a bit more testing than usual. She forwarded the info to Mac and O'Malley. The poor sod who'd likely been doing nothing more than entertaining themselves would be in for a shock when they got a knock at the door, their computer confiscated and taken in for questioning.

She turned to the shipping lanes, amazed at how much traffic there was.

It didn't take long to revisit information she'd been seeing on the large screens. She could zoom in and almost see what fishermen were having in their sandwiches. But what was she looking for? At a guess, ninety per cent of the vessels would turn out to be legit. When a ship struck her as interesting she clicked on it and instantly got a whole screed of info, including its destination port, where it had come from, and where it was registered. But what was more helpful was its cargo. Along with food there were impressive amounts of cheap tat being imported and exported. Did these ships know how closely they were being monitored? And if they did why would they take such risks with illegal trading? Quick answer, money, it had to be loads of money.

After a few hours of mind-numbing staring and tracking the screens Viv was convinced of a sequence of odd connections. So she trawled back through old footage and found there was definitely repetition in the behaviour of a small boat that was registered to Oban. Then it got interesting. A larger boat sitting static about a mile off the coast clearly waited for the smaller one to approach. They remained together for almost an hour before the large one moved out to sea and the smaller one towards Oban. Once into a small side harbour, away to the right of the main one where large boats and ferries could berth, they unloaded then sat for another hour before turning back towards the Irish Sea. There were too many boats in the harbour to tell whether there was any transaction between them, but it was odd. There was definitely a pattern. She continued to watch. Hours passed. Eventually she had enough evidence that the small boat always came and went from the south to the Irish Sea and the large one moved way out to sea. What were they moving? Frustrated by not being able to see what they were doing she retrieved her own laptop from her bedroom and began another search. They wouldn't like it but needs must. With her laptop set up in the information room she decided it was in her interest to go back to first principles. And those were to ask the questions who, where, what, why, and how? So, who owned the first boat that met up with the other vessel out to sea? Where had it been registered? What were they carrying and/or transferring to the other boat? Why did they need to do it out at sea? Whatever it was that they were carrying and exchanging, how come she couldn't actually see it? After a quick search she found that they were registered to carry fish. But if they had been, they'd bring their catch in to land as soon as possible. No one wants old fish.

She went in search of earlier data to see where the fishing boat came from. Luckily there was a way for her to backtrack to their former positions. Although registered in Oban she traced the owners back to the Irish Sea and their original port in Antrim. Whatever they were transferring had to be dodgy, otherwise they'd do it on dry land. Was it too simple to think that fishermen were illegally transferring fish? What else did Ireland have to offer that was worth taking the risk to do this at sea? A small fishing boat bobbing about in high seas had to be worth that risk and that meant money. Follow the money. The two boats spent an inordinate amount of time in the sound between Ireland and Scotland at the narrowest section. Every fisherman had a specific location or territory; they couldn't fish willy-nilly any more. So what was so good about that stretch of water? She scratched her head. There was no way that fish were worth this amount of hassle. It occurred to her that the Irish had arms. But there were easier ways of transferring those.

She stretched and glanced round the room. It definitely reminded her of a WW2 incident room, not that she'd seen a real one, only in movies. This one was more high tech. There was a large table to one side with a 3-D map of the jagged west coast of Scotland on it. In the old days someone would have moved boats around with a rake, now it was updated digitally minute by minute. No wonder the room was buzzing with electrical energy. The other two people in the room were glued to screens in the same way that she had been. Had they noticed what she had noticed or were they focused elsewhere?

The door clicked open and Mac strode in holding a sheaf of papers in his hand. He handed her the top sheet. 'Check this out.'

She took it and said, 'Yes, but look, this is interesting. I've just gone through my list of who? what? why? etc, and notice this pattern. Look at these two boats. One begins its journey in Antrim then hangs about in the Irish Sea for way too long before making its way out to this guy.' She nodded at the screen. 'He's sitting at about two miles out. These folk are obviously transferring something to him before they take off when the small one goes north to Oban harbour.' She pointed. 'See this, when the fishing boat arrives here, it docks in this area where there's something on the pier waiting for whatever it is that he's got to offload. It seems to me like an extra journey to make unless it's for plenty of money. Totes illegal if you ask me.' Mac scratched his head. 'I think this is why you were brought in.' 'There's no way that they haven't noticed this before. They'd have to be blind not to see the pattern.' Mac said, 'One of these days you're going to understand that when you're brought in it's because they want your illegal knowledge. Their hands must be tied. They want you to find a way to make it possible for the information that they can't get to become clearer.' Viv sighed. 'I get that, but it seems like a big waste of time when it's this easy. If I had some infrared camera coverage I'd be able to get a better idea of whatever it is that they are transferring. It sure as hell can't be just fish. Unless there is some serious delicacy in the Irish Sea that I don't know about.' Mac laughed. 'There's plenty in the Irish Sea that we don't know about. Our job is to find out what they are up to and how harmful it is. Of course someone must be worried about quotas. The fishing vessel is registered in Ireland.' He pointed at the screen. 'This big guy out at sea is a whole other matter . . . If we went up to the harbour we'd definitely get a better idea of what they're transferring. It would be difficult for us to go out to sea or take a noisy helicopter up with infrared without scaring them. Pity. On dry land we can use the infrared to our heart's content but you won't see the same area. You up for a trip to Oban?' She said, 'Yeah, why not. You know me – any chance to get to use new tech and I'm in.' She gathered up her laptop and went to the door, only to be met by O'Malley.

'Where are you off to?'

Mac said, 'We're going to have an early night. Trip to Oban first light. Is it okay if we raid your stores? Also, we'll need the RIB.' O'Malley raised his eyebrows. 'Do you want a driver with you?' 'Nah, I think we'll be fine. But we are going to need your infrared goggles.' He smiled. 'You have any problem with that?'

O'Malley shook his head. 'No problem. There is a tracker on the RIB so you won't be able to go anywhere without us knowing. And we've got some brand-new infrareds, state-of-the-art. Come on, I'll show you how they work.' He led them out to the shed where he opened a huge hatch in the floor and let them down into a storage space. Mac whistled. 'Wow! Manna from heaven. When did all this new tech arrive?'

O'Malley called over his shoulder, 'Keeps coming. Someone's worried about Armageddon.' He laughed.

Viv said, 'Oh my God. What have we here?' She scanned rows and rows of shelves with boxes of goodies. She could spend hours checking out this stuff. It was like an end-of-the-world-prepper's paradise.

O'Malley pulled out two boxes and handed them one each. 'These haven't even been used yet. Bring them back here and I'll show you what to do with them.'

Mac and Viv followed O'Malley to the back of the room where trestle tables stood end to end. O'Malley flicked a switch and each table was illuminated by a high wattage bulb.

'There's no way anyone can complain about not being able to see what they were doing when assembling weapons here.'

Viv glanced at Mac. 'What sort of weapons are you talking about?'

'Need-to-know basis only. But you've already had a peek at the shelves. It wouldn't take a rocket scientist to work it out.'

Viv became more interested in the shelves again. She couldn't quite make out what was written on the boxes on the top shelves but maybe she could pay another visit later and find out.

O'Malley took them through the steps of the new features on the infrared goggles. Much better magnification and clarity. The last time she'd used a set she'd been in a helicopter and it was difficult to see clearly because of the vibration. Even then she'd been impressed by what they'd been able to make out from such a distance. If these were the improved version they'd be perfect.

They made their way back above ground and O'Malley said, 'Might as well show you how the RIB works and where to keep these charged if you need to.'

As they approached the end of the shed where the RIB was, Mac said, 'Going to sea makes me want to grow a beard.' He scratched his chin.

Viv said, 'You wouldn't want one if you knew just how much of a biohazard they are. Guess how many germs you'd have exploiting your chin.'

Both men looked confused. Mac said, 'What do you mean?'

'I mean, there's more bacteria in a man's beard than in a public lavatory.'

'No way! I'd use antibacterial shampoo on it.'

'You'd also need a fungicide.' She screwed up her face. 'They are disgusting. If I were you and in the market for a . . .'

Mac put his hand up. 'Easy. I am not in any market and I'm probably not going to grow a beard.'

'Phew! Besides you're too good-looking. Why cover up that chiselled chin? Beards are for chinless wonders.'

'Why, I think that's the nicest thing you've ever said to me.'

O'Malley coughed. 'You two should get a room.' He gestured to the other side of the RIB. 'This is where you'd store things that you don't want soaked. These goggles are supposed to be waterproof, but I wouldn't risk letting them be submerged.' He jumped into the RIB and showed them both how to use the radio and where the emergency fuel was kept. 'You should have plenty. It goes a long way on a full tank. But no point in taking any chances.' He shot them both a warning stare.

Viv rubbed her hands together. 'Exciting stuff.'

Mac grinned.

O'Malley said, 'It isn't a toy and I'd like it back in one piece.'

Mac saluted him and smiled. 'Cut us some slack, we're city folk. How often do you think we get the chance to go out in something like this?'

O'Malley stood with his legs apart and planted his hands on his hips. 'I rest my case. Back here in one piece or else. By the way how long are you planning to be away?'

Mac said, 'We don't have a plan. When do you need the RIB back?'

'Twenty-four hours do you?'

Viv shrugged. 'We won't know that until we get there. We might need to track them over land.'

O'Malley looked at her. 'We could get the local police to do that.'

Mac gestured with his thumb at Viv and said, 'She's a bit of a control freak. Not good at delegating. If there's someone to track we'll be doing it. How about we keep you posted? If we're going to be much more than twenty-four hours we'll let you know.'

O'Malley crossed his arms. 'Twenty-four hours or not at all.'

Mac nodded. 'Okay, we can do that.'

Chapter Seventeen

At first light they squeezed themselves into dry-suits with neoprene socks and gloves then boarded the RIB. Its sophisticated sonar system, called a multi-beam echo-sounder, was the same as the one used by the geological survey. Viv was amazed that such a small craft had one. It seemed way over the top for a trip up the coast but it must be needed otherwise the investment wouldn't have been made. On screen they could see anything that was beneath them. It was weird looking at every lump and bump on the ocean floor as well as anything swimming around. Even a shoal of tiny fish, moving like a murmuration, was picked up. Each object below showed up in a different colour according to its density.

O'Malley warned them to avoid all red areas. 'Rocks don't give much, and the tides vary. If you get too close to the shore when the tide's going out you could find yourselves grounded.'

Mac laughed.

O'Malley said, 'I'm not kidding. Even the best of sailors get caught out in the coves on the west coast.'

Mac said, 'Who'd have thought that so much was going on beneath the waves? It's a veritable Piccadilly Circus down there.'

O'Malley raised his eyebrows and stepped back ashore. Viv and Mac clipped into their seatbelts and drove the RIB out of the bay to open sea.

She laid a hand on his arm. 'Could we go left instead of right?'

'Sure. What's on your mind?'

'Beaufort's Dyke.'

Mac grinned and adjusted his headset. 'Hold onto your hat. Oban can wait.' He hit the throttle and the force pushed them back into their seats.

He said, 'Not had this much fun since . . .'

'Okay. Spare me the details.' She gripped the roll bar and said, 'Me neither, but if we go at this speed we'll be out of fuel before we reach the trench.'

He reduced the throttle. 'You're no fun.'

She shook her head. 'What are you, five?'

Her eyes stung with the cold salt spray and she was glad to have taken the neoprene gloves from the storeroom. Moving at a slower pace meant they could see much more detail of what was below them. It was fascinating. Patches of sand were a rarity on the west coast. She realised how special the beaches were. They could so easily have been piles of rocks with nowhere to walk or picnic. When they passed other marine craft they gave a cursory wave but she was disappointed that there was no horn blowing. She watched closely at the way Mac handled the RIB. There was a definite knack when encountering the wake of a bigger boat. And although they might not be able to see them they certainly knew when something large was over the horizon, since the waves were bigger and more powerful and the RIB smacked each one with determination. Mac seemed to know what he was doing – he'd probably had experience of driving a RIB before but hadn't let on. Typical.

They passed Jura and Islay on their right but couldn't see the tops of the Paps. Everything was shrouded in dark grey cloud. They eased into the Irish Sea at the end of the Mull of Kintyre. Now closer to Ireland than to the Scottish mainland, they slowed to a crawl and, whilst visibility above board was pathetic, below the water surface it was unbelievably clear. She unclipped her harness and reclipped in beside Mac at the front.

'Oh my God. What's that?'

Massive cubes, discernibly man-made because of their geometric shape, were scattered across the seabed. Some were softened slightly by tails of seaweed gathered along their edges, others were way too clean to have been on the seabed for long at all and certainly not from WW2 time. She prodded at the screen.

Mac said, 'You don't want to know.'

'I absolutely do want to know. How the hell did they get here?'

Mac stared at the screen. 'Look, check this out.'

'Shit! That looks like some serious ordnance. But I want to know what those blocks are.'

'That's nuclear waste encased in concrete.'

'Holy shit! But isn't this where they propose to build a bridge between Port Patrick and Larne?'

He nodded. 'Since the 1940s there's been weaponry exploding and floating ashore onto the beaches along this stretch of coast to the north and south. Kids pick the stuff up and run to their parents to ask what they've found. Sometimes these are lethal weapons that were never meant to see the light of day, and in the light of day become much more deadly since they're utterly unstable. I'm going to turn the camera recorder on.' He flipped a switch and turned a couple of nobs. He'd obviously been paying attention to O'Malley. 'There are definitely some very odd shapes down there.'

As they floated and stared at the screen they heard the high revs of another engine approach from the west. The wake of the craft unsteadied them and they both clung onto their roll bars. Another RIB came into sight and slowed about thirty metres away. It was about half the size of the one that they were in and didn't look as if it had particularly sophisticated equipment on board, but it was difficult to tell from the distance they kept. They drew closer and Mac whispered, 'They don't have anything on the boat to identify them.'

Viv said, 'Neither do we.'

'Exactly. Could mean they're from another government agency, or . . .'

A thick-set man, looking a lot more uncomfortable than her in his dry-suit and with a tight waterproof balaclava pulled over his chin, shouted over to them through a loudhailer, 'Do you have a problem?'

Mac, without a loudhailer, shouted back, 'No, but thanks for asking.'

The other man shouted, his accent unmistakably Northern Irish, 'Are you sure there's nothing we can help you with?'

'No, we're fine thanks.'

The man drew himself up. 'What I mean is, you're not allowed to fish this area without a special permit. Do you have one?'

'No, we don't and we're not fishing. Just passing through.' It was perfectly obvious that they had no fishing gear.

'Well could you pass on through more quickly. This area is designated unsafe.'

'Why? There's nothing on any map to say that.'

The man reached down the side of his leg and drew out a long knife.

Viv said, 'What the fuck?'

The man brandished it above his head. 'You wouldn't want that craft of yours to come to any harm now, would you?'

Mac said, 'Now why would you want to damage our boat?'

'You can't be here. Now are you going to pass on through or am I going to see whether this,' he held up the knife, 'can do any damage?'

Viv glanced at Mac and could see him trying to make a decision. She had no idea if a knife like that could damage their RIB. They were basically in a large sturdy dinghy. It wasn't worth the risk. Mac pulled back the throttle and they began to move forward.

The man in the other RIB shouted, 'Good decision.'

Viv unclipped and made her way to the back of the RIB. She scrabbled about in her rucksack.

He shouted over again, 'Now what would you be up to?'

She took out her phone and photographed him and the driver, who was also wearing a dry-suit with a similar balaclava. The driver hadn't turned to face them, but had a very defined occipital bone, his profile sharp and aquiline. The one who'd done the talking had a reddened swarthy complexion with a broad nose and bulbous lips, the result of salt burning his skin or the balaclava being too tight, but whatever the reason his neck was indistinguishable from his head. Never a good sign.

They definitely didn't like being photographed and the driver spun their craft away from the lens of Viv's phone. Mac pulled the throttle and got up speed in case they did a loop and returned to follow them. They didn't. They took off back towards the coast of Ireland and left Viv and Mac bouncing about in their wake.

'What the hell was that about?'

'Whatever it was, that was a serious threat. No one wants a run-in with a Commando knife. I wouldn't have fancied bobbing about in there.' He pointed to the sea. 'We'd die of hypothermia pretty quickly, even with these suits on. Did you get anything on your phone that might help us identify them?'

'I don't know. We'll see when we reach harbour, although we'll not get a clear view of much in this drizzle. I knew it was a risk, but it seemed right to take their photograph. At least they didn't throw the knife at us.'

Mac murmured, 'What are they up to? If they had any official clout they'd have shown us some identification. And they wouldn't have drawn that knife out. It was some size, and it might well have gone through this.' He tapped the side of the RIB with his boot. 'Although it seems pretty impenetrable. So many jaggy rocks on the west coast.'

'The activity that I watched back at the retreat was of a proper registered fishing boat. They spent a lot of time round here then they made their way out to sea to meet another much bigger boat. They then spent a bit of time side by side as if they were exchanging goods, since I don't imagine them just stopping to chew the fat, then the smaller boat motors north up to the harbour at Oban. It stops, ties up and off-loads but hangs about for an hour or so after. We need to catch them in the act. You think those guys were protecting the territory on the other boat's behalf?'

Mac shrugged. 'God knows. But whatever is going on he was making a statement by brandishing the knife. I'm sure it was special issue for SAS.'

She raised her eyebrows. 'He could have got it anywhere . . . online.'

'I don't think you can sell those knives online . . . I'll let O'Malley know that we're stopping here for a bit. He'll not be chuffed, but there's not much he can do to stop us.'

'You want me to ring him?'

'No, thanks. I'll radio in and see what he says.'

Listening to Mac on the radio confirmed that he'd definitely done this kind of thing before. He was aware of the radio's delay and the coded language. Although Mac hadn't mentioned their location she heard O'Malley ask why they were in the Irish Sea. There was nothing that they could do in the RIB that wouldn't be tracked. Talk about Big Brother's bigger brother.

Mac said, 'Call it intuition. Do you know of anyone policing this stretch either officially or unofficially? We've just had an interesting encounter.'

'There's a gang operating out of a wee place north of Larne. Did you get anything to identify them?'

'Not much. Viv took a few photographs but they sped off. Although not before he threatened to pierce the RIB with a Commando knife.'

'Okay, so definitely not official.'

Mac turned to Viv and shrugged. 'We couldn't tell either way. He was pretty clear that we couldn't stay there legally.'

O'Malley laughed. 'If I were you I'd get back here and we can run those photographs through facial recognition. Sounds to me as if he was chancing his luck. By the way, there's some horrible weather coming in so I'd get a bend on or you'll get drowned.'

Mac closed down the radio, booted the engine and shouted above the noise. 'We'll stay in sight of the mainland. We're not going to see much in this weather. Look.' He pointed to a thick bank of low dark cloud rolling in from the Atlantic. 'I'd rather have this mist and drizzle than that. We're going to get totally overwhelmed. There's a wee shelter at the back like the hood of a baby's pram. If you want, you can pull it up and hunker underneath.'

She shook her head. 'I'll stay up front with you for now.'

The bank of clouds delivered all that it promised, a deluge of stinging, sleety rain then hail. By the time they reached the end of Beaufort's Dyke they were drenched and unrecognisable, their faces numb and bright red with cold.

Mac shouted suddenly, 'Did you hear that?'

The sound of the other RIB returning at speed had them glancing at each other.

Mac looked at Viv. 'What now? Whatever it is won't be good. I say we make a run for it. What d'you think?'

'You're the captain. You decide,' Viv shouted. 'We're never going to dry out from this. Even my bones feel soaked. Maybe we should make for the mainland.'

Mac laughed. 'We'll recover.'

'I think we should shelter somewhere like Campbeltown.'

He nodded and turned the RIB towards the shore. But the other RIB was now in sight and they seemed to be aiming straight for them. Mac pulled the throttle and sped up. The smaller craft gave chase.

Viv shouted again, 'They've swapped places. The Neanderthal is driving and his buddy, oh shit! Looks like a frikken crossbow's pointing right at us. 'Shit! Shit! Boot it and don't go in a straight line.'

Mac swung the RIB to the left, which had Viv staggering toward the edge.

He yelled, 'Hang on. This could get wild.'

The further they went, the choppier the Irish Sea got. The rain was coming down in torrents and Mac had a hard job zig-zagging to keep out of range of the cross bow. The RIB continually crashed onto the top of huge white crested waves. Grateful that she had an empty stomach, there was nothing else for Viv to do but grip on, white-knuckled, for the ride. Thankfully their craft could outrun the smaller one, but it didn't mean that their adrenalin wasn't through the roof. Eventually they were far enough ahead of the other RIB for Mac to turn to see where they were. He couldn't see them but could still hear their engine. The sound became more and more faint so he slowed down. 'We need to fill up with petrol. It's gone into the red since I booted it.'

Viv unclipped and found a canister with spare fuel. She looked round at Mac, embarrassed, because she hadn't paid attention when O'Malley was showing him what to do. 'I wasn't listening when you were being shown how to refill her.'

'Here, you take the controls and I'll deal with it.'

She kept the RIB steady but it wasn't as easy as Mac made it look. Soon they were within a few hundred metres of shore, but another red alert was on the screen showing that it was too rocky for them to land. She steered towards Campbeltown, where it was a relief to reach the protection of the harbour.

Mac stood beside her as she drew the RIB into the side and cut the engine.

He said, 'Good job. I'll get a look at a map but I'll have to go under that shelter.'

They stepped to the back of the RIB and pulled the 'pram-hood' up so that he could protect his phone screen. Both swiped at water dripping off their noses but there was no way of drying them. They huddled together to look at the map on Mac's phone.

Viv muttered, 'God, I hope this is worth it. I can't feel my face and I'm not sure my lips are working any more.'

He glanced up and grinned. 'Lips seem to be in fine form. I wouldn't worry too much.' He looked at the sky. 'Doesn't look as if that's going to let up any time soon. What do you want to do?'

'We don't have much choice. We either wait it out here until that passes, if it ever does. Or keep going knowing that we can't get any wetter than we already are.'

He pointed to a spot on the coast of Ireland on the map. 'I wonder if that's the place that O'Malley was talking about?'

It was difficult to tell but it seemed like a proverbial one-horse town, a few houses well spaced out along a tiny ribbon of road leading to a harbour.

Mac thought for a moment. 'Whatever they're doing from there everyone must know. There's no way to be discreet in such a small community. I think we should take a look.'

Viv's heart sank. 'Really?'

'Yes, "really", but you'll be glad to hear that we should do it from the air. There's a night surveillance plane with splendid equipment that we could hitch a ride on.'

She said, 'Easy. I've already done a night trip and used infra-red goggles – they were impressive. Whatever these guys are up to must be really worth it. I mean who's going to threaten another boat that, for all they know, was just out for a pleasure trip? They must have a hell of a lot invested in their goods, or in this area. So what is it? Surely not rusty old ordnance?'

He was quiet for a bit then said, 'We could take those new infra-reds up with us, although the plane also has a laser light. We could get the pilot to scare the shit out of them.' His growing excitement at the thought of a flight on the surveillance plane was infectious.

'I'm guessing since it's designed for use at sea it will be so powerful if we shone it on land we'd get our knuckles rapped.'

He grinned. 'You're right, but I think we should get back to base asap and get permission to go up on the next flight.'

'Are you sure you're not just wanting a jolly to try out the new tech?'

'Me? Of course I do. We've got to take our chances when we can.'

He revved up the RIB and pulled back out to sea. 'You stay hunkered down and we'll be back before you know it. I'll radio in to tell them to have the kettle on.'

She cracked a smile at the idea of O'Malley donning an apron and making them tea and scones.

The ride back was hellish, cold and bumpy and felt much longer than it actually took. She stuck to Mac's advice and remained clipped in beneath the canopy but it was only marginally less wet, and she had to grip the roll bar to keep her seat. Mac's skill was impressive. She'd seen what treachery was beneath the waves on the way down. It took sober concentration to keep them out of danger. Eventually they reached the bay where the retreat house nestled a few metres from the high tideline. It looked enchanting in the lee of the hill, as if an old crofter from bygone days could come out any minute. They knew better. She shivered, light was fading and the idea of a hot bath and food was suddenly overwhelming. 'I'm starving,' she shouted at Mac.

He turned. 'Me too. But I'd kill for a hot shower first. We'll have to sweeten O'Malley up to get on that flight.'

Her heart sank. 'You think we should try and go up tonight?'

'Why not?'

'Well, because they'll be on alert after our encounter with them today. They'll be rattled by the idea of someone encroaching on their turf even if it was wet.'

'And when people are rattled they are most likely to make mistakes. They might even be in a hurry to shift whatever goods they've got stored.'

'I didn't notice any large buildings on the map and that was as recent a map as Google could supply, although there were what looked like caves.'

He snapped his head round. 'I didn't notice that.'

'To the right of the harbour was a low but sheer cliff with rocks at the base right on the shore. The mouth of the cave was not unlike the one on our side.'

She gestured with her thumb to indicate where they'd been the day before.

'I missed that. Too busy looking at ways in and out of the village, and how they are most likely to travel. Which has to be by sea by the way.'

O'Malley came down to the jetty as they pulled up. 'I see you did get caught in that downpour.'

Viv said, 'How did you guess?' as she and Mac dripped ashore.

'I made sure that there's enough hot water left for you both to thaw out.'

Once inside the boathouse she and Mac peeled down the tops of their dry-suits rolling them to their waists. Someone had been having a laugh when they named them. They had to sit on the ground to help each other pull their legs free. The neoprene, or whatever they were made of, squealed as if it was animate, like nails on an old-fashioned blackboard. Viv blew out a huge breath with relief once she was completely free.

'OMG! That's like my worst nightmare.'

Mac stared at her, his eyebrows knitted in confusion. 'I don't get it.'

'No, you wouldn't. I hate being trapped, and wearing that thing was torture. I can't feel any of my extremities any more. The cuffs at the wrists and the ankles, and don't get me started on the neck, were designed to cut off the blood supply. And . . .' She began shivering in earnest. 'Don't get me started on being at sea.' She blew out another breath. 'Come on, let's get cleaned up before you start trying to fix me.'

Chapter Eighteen

She stood beneath a heavy stream of hot water, rubbing her hands and stamping her feet but not managing to get any feeling back into them. Once she'd dried off and dressed in the warmest clothes she had with her she still couldn't get any heat into her body. She shivered uncontrollably, her teeth chattered and her hands and feet were still white numb. She collapsed onto the edge of the bed and wrapped her arms round herself. She was desperate for warmth so she slipped beneath the duvet and tucked herself in as best she could. She woke to the sound of Mac pounding on her door. She tried to raise herself off the bed but couldn't move. She made a noise and Mac came in.

'Are you okay?'

Sweat dripped down her face in rivulets where her hair clung to her cheeks. Her teeth started chattering again.

'Shit! What the hell . . . Let me go get the first aid bag. There should be a thermometer in it.'

She couldn't find the energy to say anything, never mind object. She just lay there and drifted into a disturbed sleep.

Mac returned with O'Malley and took her temperature. 'Wow, it's off the scale.' He raked around in the first aid kit and found paracetamol. 'This will take her temperature down but we need to find out what's caused it. She was completely chilled on the way back. We should have stayed in the shelter of Campbeltown harbour.'

O'Malley said, 'Whatever it is, it's best to let her sleep.'

Mac looked round the room. 'We'll need to keep her hydrated. I'll stay with her.'

Viv was vaguely aware that a conversation was taking place but she was in no position to join in.

Mac said, 'I'll come down and make up a tray. One of the last things she said to me was that she was starving.'

'I'll get you food; you stay where you are.'

Mac sat on the bed opposite and watched as she tossed her head from side to side mumbling incomprehensibly. He took out his phone. 'Hey, Boss, we've got a problem. Viv's not great.'

'What do you mean, not great?'

'I mean her temperature's high and she's not even remotely compos mentis.'

'What does she need?'

'Probably a doctor. I'm not sure yet. O'Malley said to let her sleep, so we'll give her a few hours to see whether the fever breaks. It's not like her. I've never known her to be ill.'

'Stay with her and keep me posted. We've got a medical team up at Camp 16. Do you think you could make it back there?'

'Yes, if we need to. I'll let you know.'

'You realise it's best if we don't get locals involved.'

'Sure. I understand that but . . . I'll have to go.'

Viv stirred and sounded as if she was trying to say something. She began thrashing and making strange mewing noises. He didn't want to scare her, so he knelt on the floor next to her bunk and held her hand, pushing her hair off her forehead. She was burning up. She kept mumbling. Whatever dream she was having wasn't about sunshine and cocktails. He stroked the back of her hand but she became more and more agitated. He decided he'd lie beside her and hold her. He wrapped his arm across her shoulder and initially she calmed, but then began thrashing again. Jerking her head back she butted Mac on the chin. She wasn't conscious but it must have hurt when her head connected with his chin. It certainly hurt him. He held her tighter and she calmed again. Whatever was going on in her unconscious you'd never have known it in her waking life. He'd slept in the same room as her many times but never been privy to her nightmares since whenever she was dreaming she always woke herself up. Not now.

O'Malley tapped on the door and came in with a tray. He raised his eyebrows and said, 'I'll leave this here for you. I've brought a jug of water if you can get her to drink.'

'Thanks. She was thrashing about and I was . . .'

O'Malley held up his hands. 'Don't need to explain anything to me. She's your partner.' He about turned and left the room.

Once she had quietened down Mac crept over to the other bunk and tucked into the generous portion of casserole that was on the plate. He was famished and he ate far too quickly for his own good. He mopped up the plate with a chunk of bread then poured himself a glass of water. Viv stirred and began shaking again. He went back to her and lay beside her. The weight of his arm across her shoulders seemed to calm her. She tossed her head from side to side as if she was trying to shake something loose. There was nothing discernible in her mumbling. Not a single coherent word.

He searched the first aid kit for a rehydrating powder then poured some water and sifted the powder into it. It fizzed. He leaned over her and with one hand lifted her head off the pillow. 'You have to try and drink something.'

She opened her eyes and shook her head. 'No don't.'

He laid her head back on the pillow. 'You need fluids. Even just a sip will help.'

She closed her eyes again. 'Later.'

He sighed and put the glass back onto the tray. He tucked her in then lay on the bed opposite. He whispered to himself, 'Sleep might be the best medicine but what if she needs treatment?'

She did sleep and so did he. But every so often he woke and glanced over to make sure she was okay. She was calmer. The thrashing and the feverish mumblings had stopped and she wasn't pouring sweat any more. He fell back to sleep and didn't wake until early the next morning. From his bunk he drew back the curtain to a piercing blue sky and the sea like a millpond. Typical of Scotland to produce such opposites. No wonder people got caught out – you really did have to be prepared for four seasons in one day. He glanced over at the other bed. She was sound asleep. He swung his legs off the bunk and she woke up.

Confused, she murmured, 'Mac, what are you doing here?' She struggled to push herself up to rest on her elbows. 'My God, I'm knackered. How long have I been asleep?'

'Well, you skipped dinner last night and have been out since then. You've had a fever.'

She put a hand to her forehead. 'What do you mean a fever?'

'Your temperature was off the scale and you've been thrashing and mumbling.'

She smiled. 'Have you been here all night?'

'Yes.'

'What's that smell?'

He looked at the tray on the floor with the remains of his dinner on it. 'I'll get rid of that.' He took the tray and went to the door. 'Are you hungry or thirsty? What can I bring you?'

'You don't need to bring me anything. I'll get up and come with you.' She pushed herself further up the bed but collapsed onto the pillow. 'Wow! Not much energy going on here. Maybe a slice of toast and a cup of tea.'

He nodded. 'I'll be right back. It's good to see you on the mend.' He closed the door behind him.

She pulled the duvet back and tried to get up. Her legs had other plans. She had to pee so she gripped the edge of the bed, levered herself up and staggered to the en suite. Her legs felt like jelly but she made it. As she washed her hands over the basin she hardly recognised the person staring back. 'Holy shit!' She splashed cold water on her face. Dark rings had settled beneath her eyes and her skin was pale. The body is good at giving us visual clues for what it needs but you'd have to be paying attention to them to take action. The boat trip had tipped her over the edge. Two weeks of intensive training, the hike over the headland, then that God-awful weather was the last straw. She heard her bedroom door open.

Mac said, 'You okay?'

She replied, 'Yeah. Fine if you think Boris Karloff is a good look.'

She plonked herself down on her bed and Mac put the tray he was holding down beside her. 'I've seen you looking better but you were having quite the night. I'm amazed you've surfaced at all this morning. I almost sent for a doctor.'

She stared at him wide-eyed. 'No way. Why would you do that?'

'If you'd seen how much fluid you were losing and the way you were thrashing you'd have been worried.'

'I felt tired after the hike across to the cliffs and I didn't relish being in all that rain, but I wasn't aware of feeling ill until I couldn't get any sensation into my finger tips or toes. They were pure white and no amount of hot water or stamping made any difference. I thought if I wrapped myself in a duvet I'd soon get warmed up again.'

'It wasn't a bad thing to do but by the time I came to ask why you weren't coming down to eat you were delirious.'

She stretched her hand over to him and rubbed his arm. 'Thanks for looking after me. I take it you didn't go on the night flight?'

'No. You were the night shift.'

'Want to do it tonight?'

'You're not going anywhere unless it's back to Doune or Edinburgh. I think you should get checked out.'

'Don't be dramatic.'

'Dramatic. You've been over-doing it. When was the last time you had a break? I mean a proper break.'

She couldn't argue, since she couldn't remember. She bit into the slice of toast. 'Mmm. Good.'

'You must be ill when you're so easily pleased.'

There was definitely something in what he said. The idea of a few days doing nothing had its appeal and that in itself was surely a sign that she needed to rest. 'Okay. I'll go to Doune for a few nights and snuggle up with Mollie. That'll give me time to recharge. But what about the boats and their illicit trading?'

'We'll handle that. O'Malley fancies a go on that night flight. Apparently we've got some new maritime patrol planes based at Kinloss he's champing for an excuse to go up in. We've downloaded all the co-ordinates of their stopping-off places so when we go up in the air it'll be easy to home in. I think we've identified the pirates.'

She smiled ruefully. 'It's a terrible thing to be redundant. Maybe I could do a bit more digging. What are their names?'

'No. Rest means rest. Doing nothing, nada, nowt. Comprende?'

She sipped her tea but nodded. 'Okay. Doune it is.' The idea of even getting dressed seemed too much effort but she'd do it. A vision of Mollie by her side was the final push.

He said, 'I'll pack up. Get the Land Rover ready. We'll drop in at Camp 16 and pick up the Rav. You take your time.'

She finished her tea then gathered her things. When she lifted her rucksack she almost toppled over. Not an ounce of strength in her arms or legs.

The door opened and Mac came in. 'I thought you might like some help with that.'

'Okay.'

He nodded. 'You must be feeling bad.'

'I kind of am. Thanks for . . .'

He waved his hand. 'You'd have done the same for me. Let's go. There's nothing like your own bed for getting well.'

She wasn't sure that she thought of Doune as her own bed but it was closer and had the bonus of the dog for company. 'I'll ring Brian.'

'No need, I've already called him. He'll have the heating on and the dog will be there to greet you.'

She swallowed and felt her eyes fill. Thank goodness he was ahead of her and couldn't see how emotional she was. She couldn't cope with kindness when she was this vulnerable.

Chapter Nineteen

When she put the key in the door of the cottage at Doune and heard Mollie's claws scampering on the wooden floor behind it, her eyes filled again. What the hell was going on? She threw her bag onto the floor and knelt down to fuss over the dog. Mac squeezed past and walked through to the kitchen. She watched him touch the Aga.

'It's up full pelt. I'm going back to Camp 16 to pick up my car as soon as a PC arrives. You want me to fix anything for you before they get here?'

'I'm guessing Brian will have everything in hand. You want to look in the fridge?'

Mac pulled the door open and nodded. 'Yes. Everything you'll need for a couple days right there. He's even got you chocolate digestives. I didn't know that he knew you that well.'

There was more than a question about biscuits in his tone but she let it pass. 'How could I get to be this exhausted? I think I'll head for a wee nap.' She stood up but Mollie nuzzled into her hand to try to keep her attention. 'You can come,' she said to the dog.

Mac made a try for humour. 'It's all right for you, Moll. Preferential treatment or what?'

They all heard tyres on gravel and Mollie bolted to the door.

Mac opened up and waved to the PC, but said to Viv, 'You sure you don't want to give me your phone and I'll . . .'

'I'm sure. But thanks anyway. You coming by Doune on your way back?'

'I can if you like.'

She nodded. 'I'll make dinner for you.'

'No, you won't. You're supposed to be resting. I'll bring pizza from Callander. Now go to sleep and I'll see you later.'

She didn't need a second telling and made her way up to the room where she'd been sleeping since Sal hadn't come home. She patted the bed and Mollie jumped up, birled round and curled up before Viv could get in and settle herself.

When she woke up light was fading and Mollie was restless. She remembered that Mac was coming with pizza so decided a shower was in order, but first she'd take the dog for a quick stroll down the lane.

While she was in the shower Mac arrived and shouted upstairs, 'Pizza. Whenever you're ready.'

She didn't hear exactly what he said but 'pizza' was all she needed to know. She came downstairs rubbing her hair with a towel. 'Smells good.'

He nodded. 'You look better.'

'Amazing what a shower can do, although I still feel zonked and my legs aren't passing the stairs test.'

He knitted his brows.

'I mean when I take the stairs I usually do it two at a time. Now I'm gripping the rail and levering myself up like a pensioner.'

'It'll pass. Take your time.'

'Yeah. That's likely.' She plonked herself at the kitchen table. 'That said, no point in pushing so hard that I end up taking longer to get my energy back.'

'What is energy? Why do we always talk about our energy as if it's something we could put in a wheelbarrow?'

She laughed at the vision of Mac with a wheelbarrow full of nothing that anyone could see. 'Good point. It's just an expression.'

'Is it helpful though? Wouldn't it be better if we said what was actually going on? I mean, you're allowed to be exhausted after the last week of training. That boat trip obviously tipped you over the edge.'

'But I didn't feel as if I was on the edge. A bit tired, but not like I was going to collapse. Maybe it's a bug. But normally if I had a bug I wouldn't feel like food of any kind and that pizza is making me salivate. How about a slice?'

He brought plates from the cupboard then stuck the kettle on the Aga. 'I'll make coffee or would you prefer tea?'

'Tea please.'

'Ah, maybe that's a sign. Evenings are always coffee times for you.'

'God, you talk about me being super observant. What are you on?'

He slid a plate over to her with a large slice of pizza hanging over its edge. 'Here. This'll keep you quiet for a bit.'

She sampled her first bite and the mozzarella took on a life of its own. The more she tried to tame it the more tangled it became in her fingers. 'My God. I can't even constrain mozzarella.'

Mac laughed. 'Serves you right for not using a knife and fork.'

She shook her head. 'You are quite proper when it comes to food. It's pizza for God's sake, it's not foie gras. Not that I'd eat that anyway. I suppose having standards is what makes you you.' She took another bite of pizza. 'It's part of what I like about you.'

'Praise indeed. Glad that you like at least one thing about me.'

'Stop fishing. It's unbecoming. Great pizza by the way.'

They sat eating for a while before Mac said, 'O'Malley thinks that those "fishermen" are trying to raise some of the ordnance from the sea bed and sell it on to collectors.'

'I did wonder about that, but isn't it too risky, too dangerous to handle stuff that's unstable after so much time in the sea? I read that almost every week an explosion is recorded from a leaking shell.'

'Where did you read that?'

'Oh, some blog or other. There are loads of WW2 enthusiasts who are constantly chatting about what's in Beaufort's Dyke. Collectors around the world will pay for anything if they think it was rescued from there.'

'But it's rusty old, almost unidentifiable bits of . . . junk.'

'As my dad used to say, "There's money in muck".'

'I bet he didn't say that.'

She smiled. 'No, he didn't but it sounded good.' Mollie nuzzled into Viv's leg then sat heavily on her foot. Viv unconsciously stroked her ears.

Mac's tone altered. 'By the way, O'Malley watched that whole performance in the Irish Sea.'

'I suppose if I could see what the fishermen were doing there's no reason he couldn't see what we were doing.'

'He said he watched us tracking out to sea and assumed we'd make a right to go to Oban but we didn't. He was intrigued so had someone on us the whole time we were out there. He'd already alerted the Coast Guard's air and sea rescue to be on alert. He knew that our RIB would outstrip most boats since it's the same design as the Coast Guard's but he wanted to see how they played it. He said he didn't imagine they'd be gracious in defeat and thought they'd come back for more. He obviously didn't know about the crossbow but that definitely changed the stakes. Whatever they are up to must be worth a lot more money than the odd piece of WW2 ordnance would bring in.'

'And you think that on the night flight you'll get more info?'

'That's the plan. O'Malley has also got the local police on the harbour investigating the drop-off up there.'

Viv looked down at her pizza. 'I wish I was coming with you.'

'Don't worry. I'll keep you in the loop.'

She sensed his excitement. 'Yeah, but your loop and mine are two different things. I'm all about detail. You just give people a skeleton story.'

'It's usually as much as they need, but if you just fire questions at me I'll give you honest answers.'

She smiled at him. 'I believe you will. God I'm knackered, and I slept all afternoon.'

'Maybe you need to sleep for a week to catch up. Build up your en-er-gy.' He stretched out the syllables.

'Whatever. Time for me to take Moll out and then hit the sack.'

'I'll come with you.'

She slung her jacket on and they took Mollie down the drive to the lane. Half-way to the village they stopped at the humpbacked bridge and watched the river below. Viv's phone rang. She glanced at the screen then answered.

She gestured to Mac to come and listen. No one spoke but there was the sound of a car engine idling in the background.

Viv said, 'One of these days you'll find your manners and at least speak to me.'

The caller hung up.

Mac looked concerned. 'I'd feel much better if you'd let me look into those calls. At the moment they are benign. Could be some bored idiot . . . unlikely though.' He took out his phone and speed dialled. 'Can you put a trace on something? Dr Fraser's mobile.'

She stood with her mouth open. 'What the f . . . How can you get that done so quickly?'

He tapped the side of his nose. 'I have my contacts. You're not the only hacker in the house you know.'

'No, but I'm the only one who is usually willing to cross data protection boundaries for you.' She grinned.

He started humming some light tune. She linked her arm through his and they wandered back. 'I'm not worried about it but it has been going on for a few weeks now. Interesting that I didn't get a single call when we were at Camp 16. I think they must be tracking the Rav or my phone. I'm never very far from either of them.'

'It won't take long for them to get back to me. We'll find out who they are and what they want.'

'You know that morning when I was at my mum's and there was a break-in? My mum gave me a letter that was hand delivered to her door. It was a threat, a way of letting me know that they know where my family live. Then the warden was attacked and her office messed up, which seemed like too much of a coincidence in one day. As you know the local police were handling it. I wonder what they came up with?'

'You want me to find out?'

She nodded. 'It would save me hacking into the system again if you did.'

'Wow, that's two things you've let me do for you. You must be unwell.'

Within a few minutes, Mac was off back to Edinburgh and Viv locked up for the night, more conscious than ever that she was still being tracked, if not watched. She double-checked doors and windows then took the stairs to bed, the dog already trotting ahead of her. Despite feeling exhausted she couldn't switch her brain off and lay looking at the ceiling for an age before deciding to get up and go in search of something to read. In Sal's study she ran her fingers along the bookshelves. It was weird being in the very room that had made Sal the academic that she was. Every time she was in the study she got a better, broader idea of who Sal had been, the layers beneath the public Sal. We can never really know someone completely, but their books tell us a great deal about who their idols were, what motivated them and who they were becoming. Sal was organised. Her fiction was ordered alphabetically. How odd that people who worked in criminal justice loved to read crime fiction. Viv was no different. Non-fiction shelves were set above Sal's desk. Viv had already had a field day in the psychology section. No wonder Sal had been so keen to get experience at Quantico. She'd believed that the FBI were at the top of the profiling game. Viv wasn't so sure. In the UK investigating teams were encouraged to be interdisciplinary. Grateful for the chance she'd had to be on one of those teams, she wondered if Sal, who was a much better team player than she was, had given too much too soon at Quantico. Someone somewhere knew the details of what had actually happened.

Judging by the amount of coloured tabs stuck on the pages of journals, Sal had been swotting up. She'd been reading every up-to-the-minute publication on behavioural analysis. Journals were stacked according to date. The most recent ones that had arrived in the post still lay unopened in a pile on the desk. Viv had wondered about cancelling the subscriptions, but it had a finality about it that she wasn't yet prepared for. She flicked through them, scanning the subjects on the front pages. So many parallels with anthropology. One of the titles caught her attention, an edition dedicated to revenge killing. She ripped off the plastic cover and flicked through the pages, but the light was poor and the type too small. She couldn't focus and her eyelids kept drooping. She laid the journal on the desk, picked out a novel with large print and returned to bed. Moll was well settled in and she had to squeeze her legs beneath the duvet so as not to disturb the dog.

Her eyes were too tired even for large print, so she placed the book on the bedside cabinet, switched the light off and closed her eyes. But Sal's face was there, more alive than ever. As long as she was in Doune she'd be reminded that Sal's death wasn't something she could sling to the side. It deserved everything that Viv had, but she was frustrated by threats of losing her job if she upset too many people in the intelligence community.

The low growl of a car engine made her reach for her phone. From its low gear it sounded as if it was heading up the steep drive to the old house. Mollie stirred, her ears flickered and she made a grumbling noise. Unusual for anyone to be out at this time of night. She tapped her phone screen – 2.38am. The sound faded.

The room was very much a Sal space. Curtains, carpets and paintings were all Sal's kind of thing and why wouldn't they be? She thought about what she would do with it. Nothing much, was the answer, since décor wasn't her thing so long as she had her creature comforts. It wasn't time to make changes in the house and certainly not in the bedroom or study. Would there ever be a right time? The study remained as Sal had left it and had more to reveal about what she'd been up to before leaving. Sal was a planner. She was aware of there being a chance that she wouldn't return. However remote that chance was she'd planned for it. She'd planned to have the hermitage built for Viv. She'd written to Viv from the USA to apologise for her behaviour, but she'd also written her will to make sure that the estate was left in safe hands. That in itself should have made Viv question Sal's judgement, since she knew nothing about country life and Sal had understood that. The new hermitage, a Hobbit house on the top of the bank overlooking the river was such a kind thing for Sal to have thought of, but had she been planning their hypothetical future together in Doune? Viv had yet to claim it and make proper use of it as a work space. The next morning she'd go and see what it felt like. Conscious of being easily consumed by Sal's case again she'd have to be careful that she didn't become completely distracted. Ruddy needed answers and the Muldoons were still niggling.

The trees weren't yet in leaf but branches of a silver birch lightly scratched the window. Sal had loved country noises – she found them soothing. Viv not so much. She turned onto her side, pulled the duvet over her head, drew her knees up and counted sheep off the lorry back onto the hill.

Chapter Twenty

She had a few days of rest but none of those days included a recce of the Hobbit house. She was too tetchy. It was all very well researching the net, but being so sedentary wasn't her only thing. She was about to head out for another jog with the dog when her mobile rang. Mollie retreated to her bed by the Aga.

Mac's voice was welcome. 'Hi, Viv. How are you doing?'

'Feeling stronger and beginning to get restless.'

'Well, I'm ringing to ask if you fancy a wee trip up north? Nothing too strenuous.'

She sat up. 'Have you found something in Oban?'

'Well, we've found where they are delivering to and it's pretty odd. I'll fill you in on the way if you're up for it?'

'Yes. How long will you be?'

'I can be with you in an hour tops.'

'Great. I'll speak to Brian about Moll. How long are we going to be away?'

'Piece of string.'

'I mean, are we planning on being away overnight or just a couple of hours?'

'Like I said, piece of string.'

'Oh, sometimes you can be such a pain in the ass.'

He laughed. 'You're definitely on the mend. See you in an hour.'

She rang Brian but got no answer, so she put Moll's lead on and went in search of him. He was never far away.

Thankfully he was as enthusiastic to see Moll as she was to see him. The dog's reaction to him confirmed everything she needed to reassure herself that Moll was in good loving hands, and she could relax and do what she had to do with Mac or for that matter when she returned to Edinburgh. Brian and Moll wandered off toward the back drive. She watched them looking harmonious, Moll running ahead but looking back at Brian every now and again. She felt a twinge of jealousy, then the dog stopped and looked at her. It took all of Viv's mettle not to run back to her. Tears welled up but she brushed them away with her sleeve. It wasn't forever. In fact, it might only be for a few hours. Get a grip.

Mac was as punctual as she was. Something she was eternally grateful for. She disliked people who wore their lateness as a badge of honour. 'Oh, she's always late' didn't wash with Viv or with Mac. No one's time was more valuable than any other's. It was disrespectful to keep someone waiting. So, in exactly one hour, she slung her rucksack into the back of the Audi and they took off up the A84.

'So where are we going?' she said, clipping on her seatbelt.

'Before I forget, O'Malley got some local guys to keep an eye on the lorries that were leaving from the pier where those boats were offloading. And two things seem to be happening. The first is they make a stop at a large country house owned by a sheikh who is never there. But a helicopter does come in to land at the same time and within an hour of a lorry arriving it takes off. This makes me think that whatever they are transporting has a short shelf life. They don't take it to this estate and store it. They move it on really quickly.'

'And what can we do?'

Mac glanced quickly at her. 'I'm not sure yet. But the chief was keen for us to check it out.'

'Does he think it's arms?'

'It could be, but if it were there's more chance of the drop being in the opposite direction. Also arms don't have a short shelf life.'

'You mean going into Ireland instead of coming over here?'

He nodded. 'The helicopter goes to Aberdeen. Not the main airport, but a small private runway. As for Ireland there are still a couple of fringe groups who like to be prepared and I wouldn't put my money on them giving up arms.'

Viv pulled her lip. 'Is the sheikh at home now?'

'Not that we know of. He only occasionally comes to stalk. It's not the best season. He only shoots stags and the window for that is pretty small.'

'I'm impressed that you know what's in season and what isn't.'

Mac gave a brief laugh. 'Give me some credit. I did some digging before deciding whether this was worth our time or not.'

'Ruddy must think they're up to something that's beyond the local force taking it on, otherwise he wouldn't ask us to take a look.'

Mac tutted. 'One of these days you will call him that to his face.'

She shrugged. 'It wouldn't be the end of the world if I did, but I'm not calling anyone chief unless it's ironic. Can I put the heater up a bit?' She was already stretching for the controls and turned the dial to direct hot air to her ankles. She flicked through her phone and said, 'Is this where we are heading?'

He shot a look at her screen. 'Yes. How did you find it?'

'It came up when I was searching for empty warehouses near Oban. Google Maps showed that it didn't have warehouses but lots of stables. It's only ten or so miles north of Oban. Looks bleak.'

'It is a good place to do covert stuff, although having a helipad doesn't exactly say low-key, struggling budget.'

'What's our cover?'

'We're a couple of events managers looking at locations for corporate gatherings. I'm hoping that will get us enough scope for snooping.'

'Where are we based?'

'Edinburgh, but there's a London office as well.'

'What if they Google us?'

He reached into his inside pocket and took out a card. 'Here. They do exist only we don't usually work for them. I've organised for us to be acknowledged if anyone asks.' 'How posh. Do I get cards?'

'If you go into my satchel on the back seat you'll find some. There's also a cheat-sheet for you just in case.'

She stretched for the satchel and searched through his files. The cheat-sheet had key questions that an events manager would ask. The first was about capacity, real and imagined. Lots of businesses tried to cram people in. This company was too exclusive for that. They were catering for small groups – eight to twelve max. They would want to see the accommodation and menus, although they'd be more likely to bring their own chef.

They'd also provide their own security. To Viv's ears her new fictional employer sounded like they had serious trust issues, but if that's what it took to engage exclusive clients then so be it. 'Do our clients want to stalk or what?'

'The estate is only open for stalking hinds during December and January since the sheikh doesn't ever come at that time. If there was a chance of him being around, there wouldn't be any other bookings. He's a very private man apparently.' He grinned at her and continued. 'They have a grouse moor but that's accessed through another glen and has different accommodation. With any luck whoever is around today is running the show.'

'But if that's the case we'll get sent packing.'

'If we do we'll already be on site. Be prepared to take lots of snaps on the way in, especially of people if there are any. You'll need a comfort break and they will comply since it would be churlish not to help a damsel in distress.'

She took out her phone and fiddled around with the camera. 'I'm not fond of the idea of damsels ever being in distress, but for you . . .' She lifted her head up from her phone. 'Making sure we're on high-definition all the way.' Mac's satchel was in the way so she shifted it to the back again. 'So let me get this right. There is something in Ireland or in the Irish Sea that those boats transfer to a lorry in Oban, then the lorry takes them to this place, then it's transported by helicopter to Aberdeen, then what?'

'We think some of it is going to the Far East.'

'What would a sheikh be . . .'

'Oh, we don't think the sheikh is involved. We think whoever manages the place for him has a side line and that's what we're going to find out. For it to be transported the way it is takes money.'

'So it's precious to someone.'

'Exactly. Curious, isn't it?' Mac drummed his fingers on the wheel.

Viv sat up straight. 'I would have smartened up if I'd known we were going to be events managers. Look at me. I look like a shabby academic.'

He glanced over at her. 'Apt since it's basically what you are. We'll get round any questions or queer looks. You're creative.'

Mac checked the sat nav, which had gone in and out of connection over the last twenty miles. Now that they were close it kicked in. Maybe the sheikh had lined someone's pockets and had a tower erected so that he'd never be out of range. They turned in to a set of gates with a small lodge inside. No one came out to see or stop them so they continued along the exceptionally long drive. There was no fencing anywhere, but a couple of metres on either side of the tarmac had been mowed. The passing places were new. The tarmac on them was not quite as smooth as the central lane. Eventually they rounded a bend and a Victorian shooting lodge came into view. A huge parking area at the front had two small roads leading off to either side. As they drew closer a stable block on the far side of the house also came into view. The house was two and a half storeys high but the stable only one, although its footprint was at least three times that of the house. The windows and doors were smartly painted in dark grey and the walls were white. The sheikh had probably given the place a makeover. Victorians didn't do much in the way of white paint unless it was lime wash. Everything wooden was unified by the colour scheme. Nothing looked shabby and the stable block was impressive.

Viv touched Mac's arm. 'I think we should drive over to the stable block. I bet that's where the estate office will be. The house has got to be for guests so anything they're trying to hide will be in another building.'

There was no sign of life until they reached the stables, where a number of Land Rovers and two massive horseboxes with 2020 registration plates sat in a neat row outside. There was no mention on the website about horse-riding as an option for guests.

Mac said quietly, 'I wonder if they keep horses for other reasons than bringing stags off the hill.' He pointed at the boxes. 'Those are the kind of things you'd see at Aintree or Ascot. They're way above what you'd need for a few hill ponies.'

Viv smiled. 'Glad to hear you're up on your equestrian info. I was thinking that they must be for very posh horses too.' They pulled up alongside one of the boxes. 'Good move. I wouldn't mind having a look inside one.'

She continued, 'I have clients who keep horses. I mean they are serious about their horses, and even they don't have kit as grand as this.' She nodded at the huge shiny silver double-decker trucks complete with yellow flashes, tinted windows and twelve-wheel bases. 'You any idea what those cost?'

Mac shook his head. 'No, why would I?'

'Well, I can tell you whoever they belong to won't have got much change, if any, out of three hundred thousand. They're mansions on wheels.'

They climbed out of the car and walked toward one of the boxes. Out of a corner of the yard strode a capped man in his forties wearing tweeds and wellies and shouted, 'What can I do for you?' He screwed up his eyes. There was no pretence that they were welcome.

Mac stuck out his hand and the man hesitated, but finally shook it. 'We're here to have a quick look to see if this is a suitable venue for an event we're having.'

The man didn't look convinced. He screwed up his eyes again. Defensive or what?

'We're in the area for a break and thought we'd kill two birds with one stone.'

Viv almost laughed. It was so unusual to hear Mac sound like a second-hand car sales-man.

She said, 'I'm really sorry to ask but do you think I could use the ladies' room?'

The man's eyes widened. 'Well we're not really set . . .'

She interrupted him by beginning to fidget and shift from one foot to the other. 'It's getting desperate.'

He took off his cap and scratched his head. 'If you go through the stable you'll find a ladies' at the far end.'

'Oh, thanks.' She bolted off in the direction he was pointing.

Mac was right, the horses that she passed on her way were not hill ponies but beautiful, if skittish, race horses. She clicked pics all the way through, walking on an immaculately clean flagstone floor. Each horse had a large stall with rubber flooring, padded partitions, air-conditioning, running water troughs. The smell of horses wasn't nearly as pungent as it could be. Whenever she'd been in the stables at Suzy's the smell had been overwhelming and stuck to her palate for hours after.

There were six beauties, each with a stall on the left that opened onto an inner courtyard. It was quite a job to keep up with the amount of manure that one horse produced, never mind half a dozen. The stalls on the right were empty of livestock but looked prepared for occupation, with water troughs running and blankets folded over the stall partitions. She glanced right over the top of one; not a drop of poop to be seen. To give them the benefit of the doubt she guessed they'd been in the process of cleaning all morning and they'd disturbed them. When she reached the end of the stalls there was a choice of four doors. One of them had to be an office. She heard voices coming from behind a door. She turned the handle and stumbled in. Two men dressed in the same tweeds as the capped man outside looked up from where they were sitting opposite each other, both with their feet up on a large desk covered with papers, phones and screens. One of them jumped up and the other took his feet off the desk and began leafing through papers searching for something.

She giggled. 'Oops, I'm so sorry, I'm looking for the ladies'.' She scanned the room and was surprised to see a bank of massive fridges or freezers along the back wall. The other walls were covered with photographs of prize-winning horses. The sheikh was in a couple of them but never on his own, always flanked by a couple of heavies in suits and dark glasses.

'This way.' The man on his feet took her across the corridor and pushed open another door. He pointed. 'And that's the most direct way out.'

'Oh, thanks so much. This is perfect.'

The loos were actually pretty perfect: six spotless, dark wood doors, black and white tiles on the floor, not at all what she'd expect from loos inside a stable block. If they had been corporate event managers this would be the kind of place they'd be happy to bring clients, but they were not and she had to find another way of getting back into that office. She went into the first cubicle, noticing the high cistern, with shiny brass pipes and handles. She took more photographs and quickly jotted some notes on her phone about what she'd seen and the exact location. She used the facilities, came out and washed her hands, then lifted a towel from a pyramid of pure white individually rolled-up hand towels at the end of a row of pink marble basins. How odd to have loos fit for the Ritz in the middle of a Highland shooting estate. She leaned on the edge of a basin and stared into the mirror. God, she looked peely-wally. She could see the whole room in the reflection and was surprised to notice a small camera with its light blinking, indicating that it had been triggered. She looked away, dried her hands and went out the way she'd been told to go. As she passed the first stall, the man who had shown her to the loos stepped in front of her holding a large pitchfork and chewing on a piece of string or straw. She hesitated but stared straight at him then went to side-step him but collapsed. He dropped the fork and grabbed her before she hit the ground.

'Shit!' He bellowed, 'Alistair, gonnae gie me a hand?'

The office door swung open and Alistair trotted down the centre of the stalls and said, 'What did you do?'

'I didnae do anything. She wiz just walkin' past and her legs gave way.'

'I'll go and get her pal.'

Seconds later Mac arrived, looking concerned. He said, 'Is there somewhere she could sit or lie down?'

The two estate workers looked at each other and Alistair spoke. 'Aye, there's a seat in the office.'

Mac scooped Viv off the floor and carried her into the office. 'Could someone get a glass of water? Viv, can you hear me?' He started slapping her cheeks and she began to come round.

'What's going on?' She glanced round. 'What am I doing in here?'

Mac said, 'You passed out. Are you okay?'

She pushed herself up from a slumped position and said, 'I feel dizzy.'

Mac took her head and gently pushed it down between her knees.

After a few minutes she brought her head up again. 'It's the first day of my period. I sometimes get a wee bit off-colour.'

As if she'd mentioned the plague Alistair said, 'We'll leave you to it.' And the two men backed out of the room. As soon as they closed the door Viv jumped up and got her phone out.

Mac stood with his mouth wide open. 'What the . . .'

She whispered, 'This is our only chance. Get a look in those fridges or whatever they are.'

Over the next few minutes they each took different areas of the room to photograph and search. Then she slipped back into the position she'd been in. Mac had spotted a water cooler and brought her a drink. 'You really did take those men for buffoons. They didn't even bring you a drink. They couldn't get away quickly enough.'

'Oh man, the mention of a period is almost biblical. I'm sure if some men had their way we'd all be in red tents once a month.'

Mac snorted. 'Unbelievable.'

She sipped the cup of water and the man who'd been outside in the courtyard with Mac came in. 'Is she going to be all right?'

Mac glanced at Viv. 'How are you doing now?'

'I feel a bit dizzy but better than I was. Thank you.'

'I think your best move would be to get her back to your hotel or wherever you're staying.'

Mac nodded. 'Yes, you're right. Do you feel up to the drive back to Oban?'

She looked at him. 'Yes, that sounds like a good idea.'

Mac took hold of her arm and she stood up. She leaned against him all the way to the Audi and he helped her in. 'You okay?'

She nodded but leaned her head back against the headrest.

Mac said to the man with the cap, 'I'm so sorry about that. I'm sure she'll be fine once she's rested and we'll be in touch about the event.'

The man looked wary but nodded and raised his hand as they set off down the drive. Once they were out of sight Mac said, 'How are you feeling?'

'Perfectly fine.'

'Do you have your . . .'

She laughed. 'OMG! You're one of them. You'd also have us in red tents . . . But, no, I don't and if I did you'd never know.'

'I'm not in the slightest fazed by talk of periods or monthlies, the curse or

112

whatever euphemisms you call them. You forget I've got three sisters. Christ, you should get a Bafta for your performance. What in God's name made you think of it?'

'I thought I was looking a bit peaky when I went to the loo. Gotta capitalise where-ever you can. I was relying on them being macho shitheads and it worked. But we'd better get our asses as far away from here as possible, because I'm guessing since the loos have cameras they're bound to have them in the office.'

Mac put his foot to the floor. 'Hold on to your hat.'

She laughed again. 'You are incorrigible.' But on the first bend she had to grip hard onto the door handle.

'We heading back to Doune?' Mac queried.

'What else do you have in mind?'

'We could get a hotel in Oban and go over the photographs we took. And there's this.' He slipped his hand into his jacket pocket and brought out a small glass phial. 'Got to wonder what's in this.'

'Well, with that in mind, we'd better get straight back to Doune. If it's meant to be kept frozen it could deteriorate.'

'Doune it is.'

'You know the guy who I fainted for was trying to intimidate me with a pitchfork. He was chewing on a bit of string or straw and trying to look like a sub Clint Eastwood. I thought he needed taught a lesson. Odd though, there wasn't another blade of straw anywhere to be seen.' She shot a look at him.

'That's true. That is odd. I asked the guy with the cap why they didn't advertise horseback riding on their website, but he was adamant that they only did stalking and grouse-shooting. He said more than once that the horses were a private venture.'

She rubbed her face. 'D'you think they saw through us?'

Mac shrugged. 'Just before you fainted, ha bloody ha, he said if we were really interested in corporate events we'd have to take the road on the other side of the house. Guests are shown their rooms, then are given a tour of the stores. That's where all the stalking equipment is kept and it's where they deal with the stags. Pity we didn't get to check that out, but I'm guessing he was trying to get us away from whatever he was worried about at the stable. He was definitely worried.'

Viv glanced in the side mirror. It looked as if they were in the clear, so far.

'So what did you see?'

'Well before my episode.' She grinned at him, took out her phone and began scrolling through photographs. 'Some seriously fabulous horses. I've got pics. Honestly, talk about top of the range. I've got some pretty wealthy clients who invest in their hobbies, but I've never seen anything like this. We'd have to stop for me to show you properly. It was odd to have those massive fridges or freezers in the office.'

'Oh my God, you'd already been into the office.'

'Come on, this is me, of course I got into the office. Only for a minute but enough to see the fridges or whatever they are. And also photographs of the sheikh with his prize- winning horses plastered all over the walls. But then when I went to the loo, amazing loos by the way, definitely passed my test, but they had a camera that must be motion-activated. Now why do you think they'd have one of those in the women's loo?'

'You have to remember this place is owned by someone from a different culture. He'll have different expectations to us.'

'He might well have but he doesn't need to have a camera in the loo. That's just weird.'

'It probably goes with the territory if you're a sheikh. There was top-end surveillance everywhere so you were not singled out. Even the horseboxes had it.'

'I get that. I mean if you're going to spend three hundred grand on transport for your horses, and I'm talking about three hundred grand for each horsebox, then you'll have horses worth,' she shrugged. 'I don't know, but I'm guessing add a zero to the cost of the boxes. Do you know, I'm getting a feeling that this is about horses, but what could they be bringing in from Ireland that would be worth all this subterfuge?'

Mac smiled. 'We need to think outside all boxes and also find out what's in the phial.' He tapped his pocket. 'What can they need that the Irish have? And why do they have to buy it or get it from them in a way that stinks of illegal? Also it's not that big. It's not horses themselves. Could be drugs for horses?'

'Okay. That's a possibility. I'd be surprised that they'd do anything that might harm those animals though; they were like works of art. But surely they wouldn't be able to enhance their performance without getting caught?'

'So are you saying no to drugs?'

'Not at all. I'm just saying that if you've invested that much in an animal then you'd do almost anything to protect it. Remember the fuss when Shergar went missing?' She took out her phone and Googled 'Shergar'. 'Oh my God. Did you know just how much money that one horse was worth?'

'No idea, but I'm guessing you're about to tell me.'

'Fuck sake, we're talking millions and millions. Oh, but wait, listen to this, he was retired and put to stud in Ireland. Now that's an interesting angle.'

He said, 'Have you got any food in Doune?'

'No, we'll have to stop and get supplies, but how can you think of food when we could be onto something?'

'A man's got to eat.'

Chapter Twenty-One

It was dark by the time they reached the cottage. An owl hooted as Viv opened the front door. She hesitated before crossing the threshold. No Mollie. The place felt dead. It was dead without Sal and worse without the dog. She flicked the lights on, then the boost switch on the AGA which felt hot but not hot enough to cook on. Mac had insisted he'd like to cook. Said he thought better on a full stomach.

He brought a bag of groceries in and put it onto the kitchen table then he put the phial into the icebox of the fridge. He unpacked the groceries. 'I'll have something rustled up in no time. It'll help with your feeling peaky and all.' He laughed and dodged her play-punch. 'Give me twenty minutes. Why don't you go and have a bath or something otherwise you'll just bug me and try to rush my cordon bleu cuisine.'

'Fair enough. I'll take a shower. Still got the smell of too much money in my nostrils.'

By the time she returned the smells in the kitchen were a whole lot different. My goodness could Mac cook. She had been a grateful recipient a few times and each dish he cooked he put his heart and soul into. He said it was therapeutic.

'That smells fantastic. You feeling better after twenty minutes of cooking therapy?'

He took a spoon out of the pot and handed it to her to taste.

'Oh my God, how do you do that? It is delicious.'

'It's only a pasta sauce but with the right tweaks you can raise your game. I've put in a little bit of lemon, lots of roasted garlic and a touch of chilli. There's very little that can't be improved with either salt or lemon.'

'I'll bear that in mind the next time I get fish and chips.'

'Oh, fish and chips isn't worth having without the right amount of Normandy sea salt.'

'What a snob you are.'

'As I've said, a man has to eat and I might as well enjoy it. You are not going to regret letting me have twenty minutes in your kitchen, ever.'

She thought about that for a second. 'No, you're probably right, I haven't regretted it so far.'

He handed her a glass of red wine and said, 'Take a seat. I'll drain the spaghetti.'

Dinner didn't take long to demolish and they cleared everything into the dishwasher, and took out their phones. It's amazing what comes up when you have two sets of eyes on a project instead of one. She knew about the anthropological lens, that when one person takes a photograph they unconsciously bring to their selection their whole past. Journos in a war zone take very different shots depending on what their independent beef is. Mac had lots of shots of what was on the walls – photographs, a year planner and other stuff to do with health and safety at work, and bold reminders to check the temperatures inside the freezers. She had taken photographs of lots of sheets of paper on the desks and what was on the desktop screen. The only thing that was interesting was how much they cared about what happened in the freezers. Hand-written notes with red stars looked almost threatening. A note, also hand-written, was pinned to the door and shouted 'DON'T EVEN THINK ABOUT LEAVING UNLESS YOU'VE CHECKED THE FREEZERS'. So whatever was in those freezers was what they were paid to be concerned about.

'I think it's time we found out what's in the phial.'

Mac retrieved it from the icebox and handed it to her. It had a typed label with a date and a couple of rows of numbers on it, but nothing that either of them could identify.

He was thoughtful. 'We need to get this to a lab to find out what it is. But it'll have to wait until morning. I'm not going anywhere but to bed.' He pushed his hair off his brow. 'What about you, you must be knackered after all your theatricals.'

'I'm just thinking about what we're missing. Why does whatever is inside that need to be at a low temperature? Why drop it off at sea? If the journey begins in Ireland where does it end? We don't know what's in the lorries but they're large and refrigerated, too big just for phials. It might not just be one thing. They might be exploiting this place to shift other things, not to do with the owner since he's absent most of the time. What we know is that the lorry drops stuff off here then goes on to a private airfield and drops off something else. It needn't be the same cargo. You know what's interesting?'

'What?'

'It's what wasn't there. Presumably the sheikh is Muslim, but there was no evidence of his own language, again presumably his first language isn't English. There was nothing in Arabic, although now that I think of it the loos did have douches. Muslims are scrupulously clean.' She shot him a wide-eyed look.

Mac screwed up his eyes. 'I'm not following.'

'You know, hand-held showers that you clean up with instead of using a bidet.'

'Ah. Wow! Who'd have known? I've seen them in hotels abroad but never here.'

'But they are a sign that he had some input into how the place was kitted out, decorated, but there was nothing, no evidence of his presence in the office, apart from the photographs on the walls, which might not have been put up by him.' She flicked through the pictures on his phone again then looked at her own. 'Nada. Maybe the whole place is just a vanity project, tax dodge that he never uses and those guys get to do what the heck they like.'

Mac stretched, raising his arms above his head. 'It doesn't matter since we still don't know what that actually is. Look, I'm knackered. Let's carry on in the morning. We'll take that phial to Edinburgh and get it checked out. Then at least we'll have something to work with.'

'Fair enough. What time shall we set off?'

He shrugged into his jacket. 'How about I come round at 8am?'

'Okay. Thanks for cooking. It was your usual haute cuisine. You'll make someone a great husband one of these days.'

He gave her a don't-even-go-there look, but she grinned and said, 'I mean it. It's such a waste that you're on your own.'

'I could say the same about you.'

'Let's call it quits then. Night, night.'

Chapter Twenty-Two

They didn't reach Edinburgh until well after 9am. The rush hour traffic was completely snarled at the Newbridge roundabout and they sat in a jam for almost sixteen minutes. Mac had the radio on with a call-in show, which allowed people to vent about anything they fancied while the female presenter wittered banalities in reply. No wonder people's minds were numb.

'You mind if I switch this over or off?' enquired Viv.

Mac waved one hand. 'It's unlike you to ask. But by all means.'

They were both firing on fewer cylinders than usual, nothing that serious coffee wouldn't sort out. Their first port of call had been to drop off the phial at the Police lab in West Lothian. Viv had found a small freezer bag in one of Sal's cupboards to transport it more safely than in Mac's jacket pocket. For all they knew it could already be ruined. As soon as they arrived at Fettes they made a beeline for the new coffee machine. They both sipped in silence as they made their way to the NTF hub in the basement.

The room hummed with tech and cyber analysts at work. It wasn't a nine-to-five job –terrorists and other criminals preferred to work their own shifts. Once inside Viv said, 'I can't imagine this has anything to do with the NTF. It's surely way off your terrorism remit.'

'Terrorism has grown arms and legs. Basically anything that could be a threat, to people, to the economy, to whatever . . . we do what we're told to do. Follow up on the oddest things and I'm guessing whatever this is won't be the oddest we've investigated.'

'You know what I think?'

'Sadly, left my crystal ball at home. What are you thinking?'

'I'm thinking we need to make a trip to Ireland. Go to the source. Do you think O'Malley will let us use the RIB again?' Viv smiled brightly.

Mac looked enthusiastic. 'I'd thought of that. But I'm wondering if we should go over on the ferry. That way we'll have wheels at the other side. But we've one or two things to find out first. What the hell's in the phial? And if we find that out we can maybe work out the why.'

Viv took out her phone and started checking ferry times from Cairnryan to Larne. She thought of Suzy's mum and her judging horses. It sounded so benign. Ireland seemed to have a lot to do with the equine business. 'Hey, Mac, we could be in Antrim tonight. A couple of hours on the ferry and an hour's drive up the coast. Nice hotel, what's not to like?'

He shook his head. 'We're not going on a jolly. We'll have to think through our stories. Are we a couple?' He raised his eyebrows and grinned. 'Or are we colleagues?'

'You're asking whether we're in two rooms or one. It's not like it would be the first time we'd shared. We'll just make sure it's a super-super-king.' She grinned back. 'All do-able.'

'Are you really up for another trip? Your energy can't have recovered yet.'

A man shouted across the room. 'Boss! You might want to hear this.'

Mac went to the man's console and slipped his earphones on.

Chapter Twenty-Three

They chose to take the M8 and skirt round Glasgow before joining the M77 south. It was pouring with rain and the spray from pantechnicons was a nightmare. The windscreen wipers couldn't keep up and by the time they'd got to the end of the M8 they needed to refill the screen-wash. Mac, ever anal, had some in the boot of the car. Being the main route out of the west of Scotland into Northern Ireland meant the M77 was wall-to-wall lorries. Viv had asked if she could drive and Mac had reluctantly agreed, and judging by the colour of his knuckles he wasn't enjoying the ride. She glanced over at him to see if he was settling down but his brow was furrowed and he was chewing his lip. Over-the-top concern for his precious Audi or what?

'Chill. I've done my advanced,' she volunteered.

He stared at her. 'When did you get time to do that?'

She pursed her lips. 'When I was at uni. Joining the Corps wasn't an act of altruism. I knew they'd put me through all sorts of training including my HGV. Not that you'd want to be in one of those things.' She pointed to the massive artic trundling along the outside lane. 'With me at the wheel. Then there was the chance to do an advanced. I didn't get why people were so excited about all that double-declutching but I get reduced insurance because of it. So relax, your car is in safe hands.'

He rubbed his palms down his thighs and shook his head. 'Just because you've got the bit of paper doesn't mean that translates into practice, so you keep your eyeballs on the road and stop trying to convince me that my . . .'

He drew in a deep breath and let it go very slowly. 'Just take great care of my new baby.'

She laughed. 'Stick some music on and we'll be down this road in a jiffy.'

'No. Please. No jiffies. Slow and steady is just fine.'

It wasn't worth racing anyway since the ferry wasn't until 8pm.

'What's the hotel like?' she asked.

'I don't know. I told Donald to get whatever he could close to the ferry so we can make an early start tomorrow.' He dug into his jacket pocket for his phone and scrolled through it. 'He's going to send me an email with details when he gets it sorted.'

'You tell him two rooms?'

He turned to her. 'No. I told him we'd need accommodation. Not too basic. I thought we should blend in. You know, middle-class couple on a mini-break.'

'Okay, okay, keep your breeks on.'

'Don't worry. I'll be all gentlemanly conduct.' He used his RP voice for this last comment.

He was always 'gentlemanly' but she wondered what it might be like if he wasn't. No sooner had that thought struck her than she swept it aside and moved onto where they'd start in the morning. 'So, tomorrow?'

'I've had O'Malley send us the coordinates that the small fishing boat uses. It's berthed at the moment in a place called Ballycastle. But that's not where it usually sleeps.'

'D'you think they've stopped whatever they're doing because of our run-in at Beaufort's Dyke?'

Mac shrugged. 'I'd have thought they'd keep fishing. If only to keep up the pretence.' He stretched his legs as if braking, which she was already doing. They came to a halt with brake lights ahead as far as the eye could see.

'Shit! There must be an accident or road works that we don't know about.'

'I checked for road works and there aren't any. It has to be an accident.'

She glanced in the rear-view mirror. 'Yes. An accident with an ambulance trying to squeeze its way down the carriageway. I can hear the siren now.' She pulled onto the hard shoulder and those up ahead followed her lead. The ambulance passed, its blue lights and siren the only hope for some poor sod up ahead. Rain continued to lash the windscreen but they were going nowhere in a hurry and the engine automatically switched off.

Mac tinkered with the radio. 'There will be local reporting on this if I can find it.'

After a few minutes of him channel hopping she said, 'Even if we know, there's nothing we can do. It's not as if the car can fly. Oh, wouldn't it be great if we had jet packs that could take us as the crow flies to the ferry?'

'It's not that far off. I've seen some prototypes.'

'Tell me you've not had a shot in one.'

'Ever the competitor. No, I have not had a shot of one and I think I'll wait until they've done a few more trials before I sign up.'

Brake lights began to go out up ahead and she said, 'Looks as if we're on the move.' They were, but at less than thirty miles an hour, until a little further on they saw the cause of the delay – a lorry with a car squashed beneath its rear end and another car on the rear of that.

'Ouch! That would definitely spoil your day.'

He said, 'I wouldn't hold out much hope for the passengers of that first car. Sobering thought.'

'We should still be in plenty of time for the ferry.'

He nodded. 'Don has sent details of the hotel. It's called the Ballygally and it's only a ten-minute drive from Larne. Looks nice. I wonder if we'll be able to get dinner.'

'It'll be half ten by the time we get there. But they'll have room service.'

He played around on his phone for a minute and said, 'Don's really excelled himself. It's not like him to choose a four-star hotel over a hostel. He's a parsimonious soul. Always trying to keep our budget down.'

'Maybe he feels sorry for you.'

'I doubt that. More likely he got a bargain two for one or something. Still, looks good. First thing tomorrow we'll do a recce of those farm buildings that you located. Maybe speak to a few folk at their local pub or shop. They have to be known in the community.'

'I was wondering why it's such a big deal if they're shifting old weapons that have been under the sea for seventy years. Surely if they want to take the risk we should let them.'

'I had a similar thought until the U word came up.'

'The 'U' word, what's that then?'

He raised his eyebrows. 'Take a guess.'

She thought for a minute then nodded. 'Ah, that U. U for uranium that mustn't get into the wrong hands.'

'The very one. But we mustn't forget that they're bringing in something else illegally.'

'There's illegal and illegal surely?'

Mac tutted. 'You and your elastic laws. No, illegal means illegal whatever they are selling or trading.'

They could argue about this all night and so she let it go, and instead considered the writing on the dirty white van in front of them. How many white vans were racing about the country anonymously doing their thing? Maybe it was the time of day but there seemed an inordinate number of them skipping in and out of the fast lane.

Mac said, 'What's your thinking about Doune?'

She glanced at him. 'I'm not thinking about Doune.'

'I know, but what are your thoughts on staying there? For what it's worth, I think you should give it a serious shot. Maybe six months to a year before you make a decision.'

'But I don't have to make any decisions. I have a flat that I love and the only thing that is on my mind about Doune is whether Mollie would be okay in town or whether I should relinquish her to Brian who clearly adores her.'

'Just don't make any choices without giving it a real shot. It's a great place to unwind and . . .'

She interrupted him. 'What? Now I'm a stress puppy that needs a specific place to . . .'

He stopped her with a raised finger. 'That's not what I meant. But the fact that you leapt down my throat is surely a sign.'

She shook her head. 'Keep me right. I don't know this place and we could end up . . .'

'Don't worry, the ferry is the only thing at the end of the road and there'll be tons of vehicles queueing. Even for the 8 o'clock.'

He was right. There was a massive queue that would take ages to shift onto the boat. Her belly tightened. Being at sea wasn't anywhere close to her comfort zone. And even less so when she didn't know or couldn't see who was at the helm.

After much tapping on the steering wheel by Mac, they were directed to a spot in the bowels of the boat where they left the car to go up to the deck. Although it was still raining the sea wasn't particularly choppy. Massive bonus. Ferries were not as she remembered them. This one had a selection of eateries, bars and even a place to watch a film, but the inevitable sticky carpets were still a feature. If she had her way they'd stay at the front with the horizon clearly in sight.

Mac tapped her arm. 'I'll see if I can get us decent coffee. I didn't think you'd want to eat on board?'

She stared out of the window and shook her head. 'No, you got that right. I don't want food until we're back on terra firma.'

'Okay. Wait here.'

'I'm not going anywhere. Be quick.'

Three nuns in royal blue habits sat on a bank of seats close by, each one fingering a wooden crucifix round her neck. She wondered what order they were from and whether they knew something that she didn't.

Mac returned with two coffees and nodded towards a couple of seats that had the same view as the nuns'. 'Come. Let's grab those and we'll be there in a jiffy, as you'd say.'

'Never a fast enough jiffy on a thing this size.'

'I hadn't realised you were so scared of being at sea.'

'I'm not if you or I are driving. But who knows what's happening in the wheelhouse of this thing.'

He laughed and almost lost his coffee. 'I think you'll find that the "wheelhouse" is entirely digital. They might keep a wheel but it'll be cosmetic. And they'll have all that info that we had on the RIB only better. No need for you to worry.'

'Easy for you to say . . . Oh God.' She sighed. 'I'll be fine.' She looked at her phone. 'Only one hour and forty-five minutes to go.'

'The good thing is that all of the way we'll be in sight of land. So chill. We'll be across this water in no time.'

'Do you think they might let us have a look at their instruments? That would distract me.'

He shrugged. 'Worth asking. I'll go and find out.' He stood up and looked around. She joined him. 'I'm not sitting here on my own.'

They took the stairs to the top deck and pushed through a door to the outside. The rain had become more of a misty drizzle than the deluge on the way down and the sea was calm. Just the way she liked it. 'So much for us seeing land all the way.'

'I hadn't reckoned on this driving in from the west. Follow me.'

She did. He climbed over a chain that was there to prevent people from moving to the front of the bridge. As it turned out they couldn't get round anyway, since the windows of the bridge sloped right to the edge of the prow. Through the windows they could see all the displays of different lights on large screens. One of those screens was what they hoped to gain access to. Mac waved to someone inside who politely waved back. He beckoned him and said, 'Follow me.' Again.

They moved back along the deck to a heavy metal door and the man that Mac had beckoned opened it and said, 'Is there a problem?'

Mac brought out his NTF credentials and said, 'We were wondering if we could take a look at the Dyke.'

The man shook his head. 'I doubt it unless you've agreed it with the bosses.'

Mac looked quizzical. 'You sure?'

The man looked over his shoulder back into the room. 'We barely skirt the edge of the Dyke. Wait here. I'll ask.'

They stood on the deck, in rain now heavier again, until he came back and pushed the door wide open to let them in. Mac was right; there was still a wheel. She touched his arm and gestured to it.

He said, 'That's just in case some nutter decides to hack into the system or the sea is too big to cope with parking this thing and some poor sod has to take responsibility for doing it manually.'

The other man turned and said, 'Thankfully that's very rare. Can you use this before you handle anything?' He pointed to a wall-mounted hand sanitiser.

Mac went first and put his hand beneath an auto-dispenser, which spat out a blob of clear gloop. She did the same and they both took time to rub it into their hands. She looked at Mac and with her palms up said, 'Is this new?'

He said, 'Ships are petri dishes for viruses. They're constantly fighting a losing battle with new strains of Norovirus. I'm guessing that's what this is about.'

Their guide nodded but glanced around him. 'Noro among others.' He pointed to a console with a woman standing over it. 'Over here.'

Viv said in a low tone, 'Another good reason to avoid being on one of these things.'

Mac patted his hand on his pocket. A phone vibrated but it wasn't his usual one.

She stared at him as he checked the screen. 'What is it?'

Just then the woman whose console they were about to see also patted her pocket and took out a phone. She glanced around then quickly marched over to another officer and showed him her screen.

The male officer went to a microphone and made an announcement. 'Bravo, bravo, bravo.' Everyone who'd been staring at screens or the horizon shifted into action.

Viv nudged Mac. 'What's going on?'

Mac kept his eyes on the officer who'd received the call. 'Looks as if we're going to change course.'

The sense of efficiency in the room had shifted up a gear.

Viv said, 'Yeah, but what was your call?'

He glanced around and whispered, 'There's a bomb.'

She felt colour drain from her face and she gripped the edge of the desk. 'What, on board?'

He shook his head. 'No, it's in the sea and we're heading straight towards it.'

'But we'll miss it, right? They can just turn this away from it?'

He rubbed his chin. 'Don't know yet. Something this size takes much longer to manoeuvre than people think. It's not like you can step on the brakes and do an emergency stop.'

She said, 'How long would it take to stop?'

He shook his head. 'Probably about six miles. But don't quote me on that.'

Their guide came over. 'Look, you'll have to go down to the next deck and wait for the next signal.'

Mac asked, 'Which will be?'

The guy blinked and shook his head. 'Muster stations.

Chapter Twenty-Four

Mac took hold of Viv's arm and steered her out. Back on the deck Mac went to the rail and leaned over the edge.

'What are you doing?'

He stared out at the water. 'Whatever they think is out there isn't visible even though the sea's calm. Come on, let's get down to where the nearest lifeboats and jackets are.'

'Shit, are you serious?'

He nodded. 'Don't worry, we'll be fine. The Coast Guard and Special Maritime Unit are on their way.'

'Is it something that's become untethered from Beaufort's Dyke?'

'They don't know yet. But whatever it is it's a significant threat. It was detected by the ship's radar which automatically alerts the SMU.'

'How long will they be?'

He smiled. 'Not long. They're not driving massive tanks like this thing. But if they think the bomb could damage this it would have to be pretty big. We can't be talking about a box of ammo.'

'Are you thinking out loud? Could it be nuclear?'

'I'm not sure. I think they'd use a different code if they thought it was.' He checked the phone that he'd received the message on.

'Why do you have another phone?'

'It's only for major incidents.'

'Oh, well that's reassuring.' She swallowed. Her mouth was dry and she felt nauseous.

Mac said, 'Keep your legs planted firmly apart and stay focused on the horizon.'

A bell rang, followed by seven short blasts on the ship's horn, then one final long blast, and all hell broke loose. People who'd been lounging around with drinks and watching films quickly got onto their feet and started dashing around in search of officials to look after them. Uniformed staff appeared with orange life jackets on and began the difficult job of keeping people calm while sending them towards their muster stations. One woman started crying and shouting at the person trying to help her.

Mac murmured, 'How not to behave in a crisis.'

Viv looked stricken. 'Is this a real crisis?'

'How real do you need it to be? There's a bomb in the sea and we're heading in its direction. It's not as if it will remain static. It'll be bobbing around with the current. It'll be completely unpredictable. We've already changed course.'

'How do you know that?' She sounded cross.

He laughed. 'Because the shape of the headland has changed or maybe Ireland has just got a whole lot bigger than it was five minutes ago.'

She gulped for breath and followed Mac. He approached a member of staff who looked at their tickets and said they were fine as they were, someone would be with them shortly to hand out safety vests.

She watched as people rushed back and forth with children, with infirm parents; even teens who'd normally be playing it super cool were looking panicked. She grabbed hold of Mac's sleeve. 'For God's sake don't lose me.'

He tapped her hand then pointed toward the stern. 'The cavalry have arrived. No sweat.'

A RIB, much bigger than the one they'd borrowed from the retreat, was edging alongside.

'What now?'

'I guess they'll assess the danger. Whether it's still imminent or not.'

At that, the first lifeboat was lowered and splashed into the sea. 'I guess that tells us all we need to know. They wouldn't risk putting us into lifeboats unless they really had to. I don't think we're going to Ireland any time soon.'

She rubbed her hands roughly over her face. 'Shit.'

He stepped behind her and engulfed her with his arms. 'It's going to be fine. All these guys are in place for a reason. We'll get into a lifeboat and they'll take us back to Cairnryan. Then if we're lucky the ferry will be piloted back and eventually we'll get the car off.'

His special phone buzzed again. This time he answered but kept hold of her hand. 'I think we're about to get into lifeboats. What exactly is it?' He let her hand go to cup his ear against the noisy chaos. He nodded and chewed his lip as the person on the other end spoke. When he finished the call he opened his mouth to speak but they were handed life jackets and herded towards a fixed ladder. 'And we're off.'

The three nuns in royal blue scuttled past, their habits billowing behind them like sails. They could have been levitating towards the next lifeboat queue.

She looked up at Mac. 'What were you going to say?'

He gestured for her to go ahead.

'Is this really the time for such good manners?'

'Always. I'm right behind you. Keep moving.'

In the dark she descended the ladder, gripping each cold wet rung as carefully as she could. The lifeboats were lit and bobbing around in an inky sea. A member of the crew allocated seats, balancing out the weight as people filed on. There were a few grumbles from people who were not very mobile but most were compliant. Viv was given a seat next to a giant with a massive round face, tiny eyes and a red beard who said, 'Hope you can swim, hen.' He laughed. She didn't. She could swim pretty well but was in no mood to test her stamina. Mac was given a seat opposite and gave her a thumbs-up. She nodded back but there was too much noise and commotion to shout anything to him. Rain lashed the hard canopy of the lifeboat but there was no way of staying dry despite this cover. The only bonus so far was that the sea was calm. Any movement of their boat was caused by their own movement, and the slight wake of other lifeboats which began moving off, causing those still filling up to bob even more.

She kept telling herself it could be worse. There could be a force eight gale and ten metre waves. The worst thing was the incessant icy rain. The floor was puddled at least an inch deep in water and the air was cold enough for everyone's breath to condense. Everything felt scarier in the dark. She glanced around. Even though the lifeboat had a huge spotlight at the front to navigate back to the shore, there was still a vast body of water to cross before they'd reach safety.

Once they were on the move it didn't take long before the reassuring lights of Cairnryan twinkled in the distance. Most people were quiet but there was one (there was always one), a woman who thought that she was the centre of the universe and droned on and on as if she was the only person experiencing any discomfort. No one had got out of bed that morning imagining that they were in for a drama like this. The giant on Viv's left kept shaking his head. Viv kept her eyes on Mac.

Eventually the big guy said to the woman, 'Why don't you give it a rest, lady?'

The woman's lips began to tremble and the man she was with hissed, 'She's distressed.'

The giant replied. 'You think the rest of us are having a stroll in the park? We're literally all in the same boat.'

The other man didn't get the chance to answer because suddenly there was an almighty blast. The heavens lit up and the boat went into a rocking frenzy, which had them all gripping onto whatever was nailed down. Debris showered onto the hard canopy. Mac pulled Viv onto the floor. Screams pierced the night sky. Water cascaded over the sides. Voices shouted in the distance. There were other lifeboats closer to the blast. Viv thought about the nuns. Then suddenly everything became eerily quiet. The woman who'd been getting a telling-off from Viv's neighbour whimpered.

The captain's voice crackled over the tannoy. 'Stay seated, we are continuing toward the port. The emergency services are all on hand to take care of . . .' His voice trailed off as if he'd received more information.

'Mac, what the hell?'

'I'm guessing they were hoping to do a planned explosion but that sounded as if something else happened. Stay on the floor with me. We can only be about twenty minutes from the port. We'll find out more then.'

He glanced around doing a head count to be sure that everyone was still where they were meant to be. He hunkered down again. She felt sick, gripping as hard as she could onto a large metal rod beneath the bench she'd been sitting on. The giant's thick legs were tight under the bench, his soaking wet trousers sticking to them. The husband of the yapping woman had managed to quieten her down but she was still crying, her shoulders heaving uncontrollably. He spoke to her in soothing tones as if to an infant. Viv didn't feel that she was handling the situation much better. Mac had his eye on everyone else. Making sure that people were safe seemed to come naturally to him. Her body was rigid with fear – she couldn't have helped if she'd wanted to. Her knuckles were completely numb. But there was no way she was letting go of the bar that sat between her and imminent death.

Mac nudged her with his foot. 'Look. Nearly there.'

She swallowed and felt tears rising but brushed her sleeve across her eyes. A voice in her head told her to 'get a grip' but her shaking legs were evidence that terror wouldn't be quelled by one sharp reprimand. She rubbed her hands up and down her thighs to try to stop the shaking and to bring her fingers back to life.

Mac said, 'The adrenalin will have somewhere to go once we're ashore. Right now you're trapped and your adrenals need something to do.'

Tears welled up again. She brushed them away. She hated it when he was nice to her. Kindness made her want to cry and go into meltdown. She crawled over to him. 'Stop being nice to me.'

He grinned and took hold of her hand. 'You're allowed to be scared. You don't always have to be brave. I'm sorry that I didn't get just how scared you are of sailing.'

'It's not so much the sailing as not being at the helm. Control freakery at its most extreme. D'you think anyone was hurt back there?'

'I think it's entirely possible. The Marine Unit has divers who would go down and carry out a controlled explosion, but they wouldn't do that at night, so something else happened. Something uncontrolled. We'll find out as soon as we get to shore.'

She said, 'By the way, in case I forget to say later, it's official, I hate being at sea.'

'It's not forever.'

'You think?'

The boat's extreme rocking had subsided, but the wake of the explosion had sent some serious water over the sides into the lifeboat, and the pool that they were sitting in was much deeper than it had been. She got to her knees and deposited herself back down on the bench beside the big guy. He drew his legs together to make a bit more space for her.

'Thanks,' she said. 'We all have different ways to cope in a crisis.' She nodded toward the couple that he'd had the run-in with earlier. 'Be grateful that you only have to spend half an hour with her.'

To her surprise he said, 'I feel bad about saying what I did. I'd never have done that if I wasn't so nervous myself.'

She nodded. 'Don't beat yourself up about it.' She was about to say 'nobody died' but stopped herself.

He lowered his head. 'I wonder if the ferry caught that blast?'

'We'll find out soon, I guess. Look, we're almost alongside.' What seemed like hundreds of blue flashing lights lit up the quayside. Police, fire engines and ambulances all waiting to take people to safety. There were bound to be casualties. Just negotiating frail bodies off the ferry and into the lifeboats was hazardous enough. Those with children or the disabled were struggling, however much aid they received. She wondered again how the nuns were doing – none of them had youth on their side. The shaking in her legs was beginning to settle down and only a faint tingling lingered but she was freezing, her wet clothes were stuck to her and her extremities were numb. Mac nodded to her to join the others who were standing in a queue to get off. She shook her head. Now that dry land was so close she could see the ridiculousness of lining up to get off. Where else were they going to go?

She took a seat beside him and rubbed his arm. 'You do know that you're my hero, right?'

He snorted. 'Can I have that in writing?'

'Sure. It's not just your training that kicks in, is it? I mean, however much training I've had, there's no way I could have been useful. I'm okay on dry land but not . . .'

He interrupted her. 'Sure you could. Your adrenalin would have been put to good use if there had been anything you could have done, but there wasn't. We were trapped and I didn't do anything except keep you in my sights.'

'Well, whatever that was I'm pretty grateful, and you are my hero, whether you can hear that or not. And, yes, I will give you it in writing.'

Chapter Twenty-Five

The lifeboat was almost empty and they stepped up to the front and disembarked. They took off their life jackets and a paramedic handed them each a cape made of some kind of shiny aluminium and guided them towards the fleet of ambulances.

Mac stood on tiptoe and scanned the whole area. 'I don't need anything other than finding the person who is coordinating this. You want to stay here?'

'No, I'm coming with you. But surely they'll need our names to make sure we're all accounted for?'

Mac pointed. 'Let's check what they're up to.'

A line of people wearing high visibility vests over their police uniforms and clutching iPads were preparing to start some kind of process.

Mac stopped one guy and showed him his NTF ID. 'Any idea who is in charge?'

The officer shook his head. 'No idea, but my boss is the woman over there.' He nodded and Mac followed his direction. 'Thanks.'

When they reached the woman Mac showed her his ID but she was too distracted to look at it. 'You'll have to wait.' She was flustered but carried on telling her team what they should be doing.

Mac turned to Viv. 'I don't remember anything like this ever happening in my time. Even if there is an up-to-date plan of action, there has to be someone to execute it. No easy task.' He took out the phone. 'I'm not supposed to use this but . . .' He punched a single digit and waited. When he spoke he said, 'I think this constitutes an emergency. I am on the quayside at Cairnryan uninjured, what should I be doing?' He nodded as the person on the other end spoke. 'Okay, okay, okay.' He finished the call and raised his eyebrows. 'It's not good. A fishing boat has been blown up. They don't imagine any survivors from that boat but the ferry was also damaged and it could take days to bring it back to shore. We'll have to find another way home.'

Viv said, 'Once we let the right people know that we are okay we can head over to the other dock and hitch a lift from a lorry going north.'

His frowned. 'I guess that's a possibility. I had thought we'd find a police vehicle but you're right, they'll all be tied up. Let's go and find our names and get ticked off.'

They snaked through the throng of service vehicles and people until eventually they found someone willing to let them go. They both understood the efforts that would be put into recovering them if they left without being accounted for. Once that was done they made their way to the other terminal to find a taxi, or if pushed, Mac could flash his badge again and hitch a lift. Everywhere was chaotic and Mac seemed to be actively side-stepping every port authority official. Not a chance of a taxi so Mac spoke to a lorry driver who'd stopped to secure his load. The heavy-set driver stared at them, obviously took pity and said, 'Hop up. Looks as if your night couldn't get much worse. I'm going to Glasgow via the A75. Have to weigh-in on the M74.'

Mac looked at Viv but she wasn't paying attention. He nodded. 'That'll do.' They removed their capes. Viv turned hers inside out and climbed up and laid it on the seat. She didn't want his faux fur seats to get wet. A fan blasting out hot air and a neon light announcing Shuggie was aboard couldn't have been more reassuring.

For the first few miles Shuggie and Mac chatted about what had happened but then they fell silent and Shuggie switched his radio on. The BBC News already had a story about a mine exploding in the sea off the south-west coast of Scotland. No details but casualties expected. Mac looked at Viv. 'You don't suppose those casualties could be our guys?'

She shrugged. 'Karma?'

As they approached the services at Abington, Mac said to the driver, 'You couldn't find another lorry leaving the services going to Edinburgh on that thing could you?' He pointed to an illegal air-band radio.

The driver grinned and took up the microphone. Abington was an hour from Edinburgh; quicker for them to get home from there than if they went to Glasgow and had to find a train back. The second lorry was half the size of the first, which meant they were squashed into the front with the new driver, who was less obliging than the first. But what the heck, it was only an hour before they reached Hillend and Donald, Mac's secretary, was waiting in the bus terminus to collect them.

'Thanks for stepping up, Don. Let's get Viv home. You know where to go.'

Don nodded. 'Did you get word of what it was?'

Mac said, 'We heard on the BBC News that it was a mine.'

Don sniffed. 'Good story.'

'You can fill me in once we drop off Viv.'

She was about to object but stopped herself. There was nothing she could do so it didn't matter if she knew the whole story immediately. She could check once she'd had some sleep.

She said, 'I think I'll sleep in the West Bow then in the morning head up to Doune for a couple of nights.'

Mac nodded. 'Good call. You want a lift?'

'I'll take the train. It'll be an adventure.'

'Glutton for punishment or what?'

'All will be well.'

Chapter Twenty-Six

The morning brought pale blue skies and a bitter wind to the West Bow. A stark feeling of exhaustion and dread that perhaps she didn't belong anywhere hung over Viv. She'd had one of those dreams where she'd been running through water up to her waist and couldn't get her legs to move fast enough. Something was chasing her, nothing specific, something shapeless but animate; even when she tripped and staggered it didn't catch her up. She hauled the duvet over her head and tried to snuggle back into the pillow but it didn't work. She threw the duvet back and looked out of the window over Greyfriars kirkyard and the ornate turrets of Heriot's School. There were worse skylines to wake up to. She headed for the loo. She felt torn. Her future was surely urban – it was where she was most herself. But the self wasn't fixed and she was not the kind of person to remain static. In her world static was too close an ally to dogmatic. But Doune was Sal's territory and she'd often felt like an extra in the wrong movie when Sal was around. Now she worried she'd be a trespasser. She reminded herself that because a place was comfortable did not make it comforting. It was alien for her to feel quite so at sea.

Once she'd packed a couple of big jumpers, her old walking boots and a few other bits and pieces she was ready to head out. As she locked up Ronnie came out of his door.

'Hi, Ronnie, how are you doing?'

'Fine thank you. You?'

'Yeah, okay. A bit hectic but fine.'

'You've had a couple of visitors.'

She turned to look at him. 'They didn't leave a calling card.'

'They looked official. Wore dark suits.'

She shrugged. 'Mormons or Jehovah's Witnesses maybe?'

From his expression he hadn't thought so, but doubted his own assumption.

'If they're desperate they'll come back.'

'What if they ask . . .?'

She smiled and said, 'Don't you worry about them. As I say if they really want me they'll find me.' Ronnie knew nothing about her life beyond the hours she kept in the West Bow. He'd known Sal was the owner of the flat before Viv bought it, but he didn't know that they'd become close, and the less he knew the less he'd have to tell when people did come asking. 'Good to see you. I'm glad you're well.'

He might have been about to say something else but she smiled again and waved as she took the stairs.

When she arrived at the cottage it was cold and needed aired. She flung open a few windows but turned the AGA on full blast and lit the wood-burner. The place was desolate without the dog but she had things to do before she'd collect her. Next on her list was to go to the Hobbit house and spend a bit of time setting up in preparation for working there. If she didn't feel a sense of belonging there was probably something she could do to change that, and a decent working space with all the tech that she had in Edinburgh would go a long way to helping. She'd brought her favourite cup and saucer but she'd need a small kettle for on top of the wood-burner. How Brian had managed to put such a small stove in was a miracle, but necessary to keep the space warm. The place smelled of newness, which was no bad thing since she could put her own stamp on it without worrying that she was doing anything to upset Sal. She took out her phone to test the signal. Three bars, plenty to order a new adjustable seat to go at the built-in desk that Brian had made, a rug and a small kettle. She wondered about bringing some books from home but for now she was happy with her Kindle App and Google. It wasn't as bright a day in Doune as it had been in Edinburgh, but it wasn't raining or windy which was a bonus after the shenanigans of the last few days. She rang Brian and asked if it was okay for her to see Mollie.

Within ten minutes he was at the cottage with Moll who went into a spin as soon as she saw Viv.

'If only humans knew how to give that kind of welcome,' she laughed.

'If they did we'd take what we get from dogs for granted.'

'Oh, it's so good to see her.' She was kneeling on the ground and the dog jumped on her and pawed her as if she'd been gone forever. 'Thanks for letting me have her. I'm probably only around for a couple of days but it'll be great to have her company.'

'She'll love having you all to herself. With me she has to compete with the other dogs for my affection.' Brian handed Viv a lead. 'She's pretty good at recall now so I'm not sure you'll need it, but use it if you're worried about her taking off.'

'Thanks. I'll ring you when I'm going back.'

He set off down the drive and Moll didn't give him a second glance. She raced into the cottage and straight to her bed by the AGA. Dogs know when they're onto a good thing. Viv pottered around the kitchen checking cupboards for things she might turn into a tray-bake. Amazed by the amount of dry ingredients that were still within their sell-by date she set about concocting. With butter and treacle melted and muesli and cranberries stirred in she pressed the mixture into a tin and stood back and admired it before storing it in the fridge. If she left it too long she'd have talked herself into doing quality control, thereby leaving a paltry amount for later. She wasn't a cook by anyone's stretch of imagination but with those ingredients she couldn't go wrong. A layer of chocolate on the top would be the finishing touch. If she had the energy she'd shop for it later.

She took the stairs up to the bedroom with the dog at her heels. Her legs were definitely not passing the stairs test yet. She crawled beneath the duvet and Moll snuggled up at her back. They slept soundly until she woke up with a start. Disoriented she flung her legs over the edge of the bed and grabbed a dressing gown. Moll followed at a clip. They hurried downstairs where Viv slipped on her boots and they both ran out to the drive. When they reached the gates she could see a large 4x4 parked at the side of the old house. The people who rented it worked in the film industry and came and went but they hadn't been around much that year. Maybe they were back. She returned to the cottage for breakfast. Coffee tasted different in the country. It must be the quality of the water. Less chlorine would do that. Edinburgh used to be known for its fabulous clean water but these days it often had a slight chemically smell as it came from the tap. The estate had its own wells, no doubt chlorine-free.

Still in her PJs she went back into Sal's study, stood with her hands on her hips and thought about how Sal might hide something. The last time she'd been raking around in here she'd been too focused. Now she had to take time, be open-minded and something would emerge. She'd been obsessed with what she'd find on Sal's computers and she'd had a limited time before the NTF arrived to take them away. Now that all Sal's tech was back in place she could go through it at her leisure, but she also wanted to sweep the room more thoroughly. She was convinced there had to be something that would give her information about Sal's death. What exactly had Sal been working on before her trip to the USA?

She was still in denial. Surely Sal would one day just walk in the door? At some level she knew this wasn't going to happen, but the only way to move beyond that was to find evidence that Sal's death was absolutely true. She'd gone over and over in her head the vision of Sal that she'd seen in the mortuary in Virginia; the body looked like Sal but not like any Sal Viv had experienced. She wished she'd asked to see more of her – even her hands and feet would have left Viv with a more complete image. She'd spent nights convincing herself that it had to be Sal, but what if her gut was right and it hadn't been? She hadn't spoken to anyone about this doubt but she'd hacked into every site that Sal had researched on her computer to look for clues to back up her theory. When she'd received the first of the silent calls, she'd longed for it to be Sal. Then reason had kicked back in and she told herself off for fantasising. It was much more likely to be one of the Muldoons' goons trying to put the frighteners on her for interfering in their 'work'. Chasing a thief was instinctive; it wouldn't have occurred to her not to. She could live with the calls as long as they didn't escalate into anything more threatening.

She sat on the floor with her back against the only section of wall without shelves and began going through Sal's books, flicking them open to see if anything fell from their pages and checking for chapters with underlined words and sentences. This would take a while but she was in no hurry. She tried to keep on task although it was easy to get side-tracked. There was so much overlap between psychology and anthropology. Sal had a number of books that Viv had read for her own degrees. Books on palaeoanthropology, how early human physical development went hand in hand with our psychology, the emerging of language communication, the importance of the reptilian brain – fight or flight was still a mantra of behaviourists today.

Eventually, when her butt was too numb to continue, she stretched and decided to take a shower, then have a proper walk with Moll who lay patiently at her side. Just as she was about to head down the drive her mobile rang. It was Mac. 'So, you want to know the results from the lab or the story of the fishermen first?'

'The fishermen. Were they our guys?'

'Well, that's the thing. They haven't been able to identify the body parts yet, but the boat was definitely the one we'd been tracking. They were after the spoils of Beaufort's Dyke and were trying to access the concrete block with the waste in it.'

'What, the nuclear refuse?'

'Looks that way. They had some heavy winching gear on the boat that was too big just to trawl their nets. The size of the chain that's been found still looped over one of those concrete cubes is industrial. So far the Marine Unit think that the boat was trapped by the chain. Those cubes weigh more than their boat, more than seven tonnes. I don't know what they were hoping to do. One thing though, they'd have to have been staring constantly at their screen not to see that a huge mine was floating towards them. I'm speculating. There'll be a massive enquiry, which will take forever to find out what really happened. But for now I think the trade to our equine estate is small potatoes.'

'And talking of equine estates what about the phial?'

'Semen. Not horse semen, though. A prize bull's.'

She snorted. 'What the hell? You think if we'd picked up a few phials they'd all have contained the same, or might the trade be in the semen of anything that's won a prize or the Derby?'

'We might laugh, but apparently to have a prize bull leads to mega bucks. This particular semen belongs to . . .'

'Oh, my God, the bull probably has a name and a passport.'

'It certainly does and if you'd let me finish you'd know that name. He's called Trueman McJagger – some farmer with a sense of humour. The number on the side of the phial was his passport number so it was relatively easy for the lab to trace him.'

'Wow. There's a whole other world out there that us townies have no clue about. But I take it our fishermen were trading that as a side-line to their fish and munitions?'

'Oh, I think that they'd make more money from a little phial from Trueman McJagger or a Derby winning race horse than they'd make from fish. However, if they managed to get their hands on any of that nuclear waste they could have retired on the proceeds. Now the issue is whether or not the blast from the mine damaged any of those concrete shells. There are special diving teams down as we speak.'

'Amazing that eugenics is still alive and well. Why is it that one particular bull or horse or person for that matter is deemed superior?' She scratched her head. 'People seem to be intent on making their lives more complicated. I mean why would they take so many risks? I know, I know it's about the money and prestige, but really? I wouldn't spend a second more at sea than I absolutely had to.'

He laughed. 'There are people who were born to be at sea. As for people making their lives more complicated, you're one to talk . . . You thinking about taking a break any time soon? Bahamas? Get some colour in those cheeks.'

'Not a chance. Flying is a bit like sailing, fine if I was at the controls but otherwise nah. Keeping my feet on the ground. What happens now?'

'I'm guessing we'll be told to stand down. Let the Marine Unit sort out the mess in the Dyke and in Ireland. As for the semen that will be handed over to the Department for the Environment, Food and Rural Affairs,

DEFRA for short. You might need to know about them sometime, what with you being a landowner and all.'

'Just as well you're not within whacking distance.'

He continued, 'DEFRA will soon have a team checking those freezers. There's lots of illegal trade, you know, small stuff that they'll turn a blind eye to, but they're not keen on anything that crosses a national border, especially if it has genes. They'll crack down on stuff that can be grown – seeds of any kind.'

She scratched her head. 'God, you have to admit that this has been a weird one, even for us. Still back to rural reality and I'm guessing that Moll is champing to get out. Catch you later.'

Chapter Twenty-Seven

She and Moll stood on the porch trying to decide which way to go. However the sound of a machine drew her towards the front drive of the old house. Brian was sitting on a ride-on mower wearing ear-defenders, moving away from her. She trotted to catch him and he almost jumped off the machine with fright.

'Sorry, I didn't mean to scare you.'

'No, you're all right. I just get into the zone. My own wee world and forget that there are other folk around. How are you doing?' He turned the engine off and crouched down to scratch Moll's ears.

'We're fine. Needed some fresh air.'

'Mac said you were under the weather.' He looked up at her.

'I'm fine. Knackered, but otherwise okay. That looks like quite good fun.' She pointed to the machine.

'It is. But it gets monotonous once you've been at it for a few hours.'

'I'd be happy to have a go if you've had enough.'

He hesitated before answering. 'You're supposed to be resting.'

'Has Mac been on at you to watch me?'

He looked away. 'I can show you how it works, then next time this needs scarifying when you're around you can do it. But only this section, mind.' He showed her how it had to be switched on from cold and how to lift and adjust the harrow on the back. It worked while in reverse, which sounded cool and risky. Once they'd gone over everything she'd need to know he showed her where the petrol was kept to top it up. 'I'd prefer if I was around when you start it but . . .'

Viv flapped a hand at him. 'Don't worry, I'll give you a call. I wouldn't take your machine out without you knowing. Besides, I've already forgotten how to start it.'

He smiled and nodded as he got back on the machine and started it up. With Moll capering about impatiently, Viv waved and wandered off past the old house and down the back drive to a large overgrown pond. It was surrounded by cute looking beehives with pointed roofs, and had a couple of small islands in the middle with arched wooden bridges which allowed the bee-man to feed his charges and gather their honey. It looked as if fairies had taken up residence. She continued down the drive lined with vast mature trees and verges with the beginnings of all kinds of daffodils peeking through. Someone in the distant past had had a vision of how this would look for future generations and it worked.

A loud crack came from a thicket of conifers on her left. She turned quickly, her heart thumping in her chest. It happened again. Moll pulled on the lead, her nose moving wildly from side to side. Then she spotted the white rump of a roe deer disappearing into the wood. She took a deep breath and gave herself a talking-to. She was in no danger. The phone calls were just that. Calls to keep her on edge. If she remained on edge they'd won. She took out her phone and checked her messages; three from Jules, but none that was urgent. She veered off to the left and joined a path to the river. When she ran this route she didn't notice anything, but now that she was walking she saw birds and ducks that she couldn't identify. The river meandered way into the distance, each side lined by mixed foliage, gorse and ferns competing for domination. She thought about how many times Sal had walked this path and how crazy it was that she wouldn't ever again. How could that be? Maybe being here was a bad idea. Maybe being surrounded by Sal's possessions was preventing her from getting perspective. She had to go through whatever stages of grief were necessary, there was no way of avoiding them, but the stages weren't linear. She was regressing. Would she do that if she was in her own flat in Edinburgh? One way to find out. Besides the bandwidth was better in town. She could get some work done at the cottage but not as easily as in town. How easily she could talk herself into and out of anything.

Once Viv and Moll reached the chapel they retraced their steps but, instead of using the path back to the drive, they continued along the riverbank. There was a public park on the other side of the river, used by joggers and dog walkers, but it was rare to see someone on their own loitering unless they had a fishing rod in their hand. People didn't loiter in the countryside, but she definitely spotted a man leaning against a tree on the opposite bank. What was he doing? He was too far away to see clearly, but as she drew closer he pushed himself off the tree and walked in her direction. He was staring but so was she. It became a contest of who would break eye contact first. Not her, even if it meant getting a crick in her neck in the process. He was dressed in black, also unusual for the country walker. She was getting the hang of the cultural nuances of city versus country. In the country people blended in, if not because they consciously wanted to but because tradition dictated it. She stuck out the same way that he did. Her black jeans and townie jackets prevented her from blending in. He stopped, so she stopped. He crossed his arms, so she did too. WTF? He could just be a guy out for a walk who was as annoyed with her for staring at him as she was with him. He nodded. She shouted to be heard above the rumbling of the river, 'Can I help you?'

He grinned and shook his head, then threw her a wave of dismissal and walked on. She felt stupid, infantile. What the hell was wrong with her?

Mollie hadn't reacted to him at all and kept busy with her nose to the ground. Viv looked at his retreating back then at the dog and realised she should take a leaf out of her book. What was it about this bloke that had caught her attention? There had to be something. His body language was not that of someone who was simply out for a stroll. She turned and headed away from the river towards the cottage, the dialogue in her head going full tilt. 'You're imagining things; not every guy in black is a bogey man. Get your shit together girl or you're gonna end up institutionalised.'

There was a package on the top step of the porch, addressed to her. Mac was the only person who knew she was in Doune and he wouldn't be sending her gifts. To get in she had to shift it to one side with her boot. It was light and it slid beneath the wood store. She left it and took Moll inside, wiped her paws down then washed her hands and put the kettle on. There were many ways for people to get inside her head but she had to create the terrain for them to do it. She phoned her mum. It rang and rang, then went to the answering machine. She didn't leave a message but checked the time. Her mum could be at lunch or at some activity in the pound. The kettle boiled, so with a mug of tea in hand she went up the stairs with Moll at her side into Sal's study to continue her search. This time she was going deep and dark, as if firewalls were a thing of the past.

Whoever had looked over Sal's computers at the NTF had been thorough but not overly worried about leaving their own footprint behind. Why would they? They wouldn't imagine anyone using Sal's computers again, probably imagined they'd be sent to the crusher, so no need to clean up their leftovers excessively. Viv could trace every action they'd taken. They'd been invested in Sal's visits to Quantico and related sites but there wasn't anything there that Sal shouldn't have been looking at. She'd been working by the book. If only she could get her hands on the laptop that Sal had used when she was in the US. There was no way the FBI were ever giving that up.

Her mobile rang. 'Hi, mum, did you check your ring-back service?'

'No. I was out in the corridor speaking to Mrs Cheng Jung and heard the phone ringing. I was hoping you'd call.'

'How is the warden?'

'She's fine. A bit shocked but fine.'

'Was anything missing?'

'Not that she could see. It seems as if they were here to emphasise their message.'

'Wow, did they ask her for information?'

'Yes. But she had nothing to give. I'm guessing she gave him some grief and he whacked her for her cheek. Overkill, wouldn't you say?'

'Indeed I would. If they want to get to me they only have to come to the West Bow. Or catch me parking in the Grassmarket every day. What do you think their real message is?'

Her mum paused for a moment. 'Well, I've been giving it some thought and remembered that your dad had the odd run-in with the Muldoons. In the end one of them did time.'

Viv let out a breath and thought, yeah that would do it, but she said, 'I'm guessing that whoever that was is no longer around. I mean it was a long time ago.'

'It was. But when the next in line steps up they might think it's their duty to settle old scores.'

'What? So they're coming after me because of dad?'

'It's a long shot but . . . could be. But what else do you think it is about? You must have some idea.'

'I had no idea when I chased that thieving guy in the Grassmarket that I was opening a can of old worms. Besides, everything happened too quickly. I called the police at 8am-ish and came round to see you at about 11.30am. That wasn't much time for them to find out who I was, then set up those threats, although the calls had been happening before that.'

'What calls?' She spoke sharply.

'Just calls where no one speaks. Nuisance but . . .'

'Maybe they have had an eye on you and it just took a little time for you to step on their turf.'

'As you say. Overkill doesn't cover it. But what can they hope to gain from me?' Viv rubbed her forehead.

'If they have your number they already know more about you than you'd like them to. And there's no accounting for old revenge. We're not talking about a rational bunch of people.'

'Seems a bit of a stretch to think there's a major trans-generational feud going on out of the blue.'

'Oh, these criminal dynasties are precarious in the extreme. They will use the past to make themselves more powerful in the present. We're talking about tender egos looking for ways to gain command.'

This made sense, but Viv wondered what exactly her dad had done to keep a family on her tail for so long when they could have harmed her many times before now. She had to find more on the Muldoons and that required more digging. 'Do you know much about them and what dad did?'

'A little, but I'd advise you to leave well alone. Not that you'll pay any attention to what I advise, so when you're next in town drop in and I'll see what I can dig out. I'll have to go. James is coming for a visit this afternoon and I've not got any treats in for him.'

'Right. I'll see you soon.' Her mother was not a 'treats' type of person, or she'd never been with her and Amanda. Maybe she was softening in her old age. But as soon as that thought occurred to her it didn't ring true and she batted it away – was this the project she needed to give her space from fretting about Sal every hour?

Time to start unearthing what her dad had been up to. First stop in Edinburgh would have to be the National Library – old newspapers online would have information on cases that her dad had been involved in. But for now she had to think about whether she could bear to leave Moll with Brian or take her into town. She retrieved the parcel from the porch. She smiled when she opened it and a small personal alarm fell out with a note from her mum. It said, 'Always better safe than sorry.' Maybe an old leopard can change its spots.

Chapter Twenty-Eight

On her way back to Edinburgh she took the turn off to Hopetoun, the route that avoided all the snarl-ups through Corstorphine. As soon as she'd spotted the view of the Castle and Arthur's Seat from the motorway she felt her confidence rising. She checked herself. Did familiarity breed contempt? She wasn't sure, but thought the saying was contemptible in itself. With the image of the Muldoon from the Grassmarket etched on her mind, she couldn't believe she'd let her guard down, just because she was familiar with the city. She heaved a sigh. It was good to be home, although she felt a pang at not having Moll with her. She wove through the north into the city. The richest and the poorest lived cheek by jowl, in some areas less than a stone's throw away from each other. A win-win situation for any city economy. Regular burglaries meant higher insurance, more high-tech surveillance, superior car alarms and tracking systems, none of which stopped those in desperate need of their next fix. She'd once been told by a cop that if you wanted to prevent a break-in get a yapping dog, since they're less motivated by food and not so easily bought off.

As she pulled up at the next traffic lights an alarm was going at a bungalow on her left. The blue light on its alarm box was flashing but there wasn't a single person in sight. Although she couldn't see the back of the house from where she sat, it was overlooked by other bungalows. Most criminals were a few steps ahead of alarm companies since they'd discovered there was very little that a can of expanding foam wouldn't sort out. The car in front stalled and she missed the change of the lights. She stared at the completely ineffective blue flashing light and smiled, wondering if there was a terrier inside that she couldn't hear. By the time she moved on she'd been stationary for about six minutes and any self-respecting burglar would have got in and out in that time. Not that there was any sign of movement.

She parked at the bottom end of the Grassmarket and pulled her hood up against a shower of rain. It felt like a long time since she'd been home. She grabbed her bags from the boot and pressed the fob to lock the Rav. She nodded to Bella through the window as she passed and Mo stood in his doorway looking up at the sky.

'Ah, Doctor Fraser. If only I could offer you some help with those bags. No one here to watch the shop. You could leave one and come back for it.'

Viv smiled. 'Thanks, Mo. But I'm on it. Not too far now.' After Viv had had a dalliance with a man who lived in the building next to Mo's shop he'd called her Doctor Fraser. Before that she'd been pretty anonymous, or known as the woman with the chocolate digestive addiction. She'd asked him to call her Viv but he liked the fact that she was a doctor, although he'd never asked of what. Once inside the flat she pulled up the windows to freshen the place but quickly realised that she'd been over-enthusiastic and pulled them down again to just let a slight draught in. She lit the cupboard downlighters and booted up her computers. While waiting for them to come to life she nipped back downstairs to collect her mail from the pigeonhole in the front passage. Most of it was junk which she discarded into a new communal recycling bin, and she took what actually had her name on it up to the flat. She flicked through it as she went. The only things of interest were a letter from her new solicitor and one from the university. Neither could be urgent so she dumped them on her desk and retreated to her tech cave.

She usually started her research in a perfectly legal way but if that failed, dug deeper, sneaking past protection as if it was a cheap voile. The National Library had screeds of newspapers digitised, which, although valuable, could be a time sap. But knowing a vague timeline when her dad would have been in a position to nick one of the Muldoons should make the search easier. The difficulty with being a researcher was knowing when to leave something alone.

Doubly hard since her dad had clearly been busy and so many tantalising stories came up with his name on them. Eventually she found the story that she imagined she would. A *Scotsman* headline of a body washed up on the shore behind Granton gas works. It had been a murder with a signature, the hands of the poor man had had wooden dowels driven into the palms, a modern day crucifixion. Her dad had been the leading detective on the case and, according to the journalist, he'd given out the same kind of platitudes then that we'd expect today. 'We'll leave no stone unturned', 'Must find justice for the man's family' etc, etc. So her dad had publicly alerted the people who'd carried out the murder. No way to hide who was leading an investigation. Even now there were specific detectives who were regarded as the most worthy opponents to specific Edinburgh criminals. This world was new to her. She'd gathered quite a bit about Edinburgh's establishment on an earlier case, and realised how thin their veneer of sophistication was. But these old family dynasties, as her mum had called them, were something else. Old school needn't be an honourable thing. The first article read like a work of fiction but it gave her more info to track. It seemed that not only detectives were prey to becoming worthy opponents, being a lawyer was also a risky business, especially if forced to defend any of the criminal underworld. After her conversation with Diana she couldn't imagine a sane lawyer taking on their work willingly. Although willing was probably the wrong word. Diana said most lawyers would avoid them but some had been blackmailed or threatened to comply, then once in their pay it was difficult to get out.

Viv had a lot in common with criminals who dug the dirt on people then kept it as leverage. Her head was full of snippets of gossip that, used out of context, could ruin a reputation. Luckily her criminality was light-weight, or so she liked to think. Once she had names and photographs she could match them to any social media presence they had. So much could be gleaned from an innocent Facebook profile. Know thine enemy. So with her head down she continued to scroll.

Chapter Twenty-Nine

Her phone rang. At first she thought it was another silent call but a male voice said, 'I'd be happy to come over to you any time. How about now?'

'Who is this?'

The man laughed. 'Ah, the card says anonymous sex.'

'I think you've misdialled. Try again.'

'Are you Vivacious Vivian?'

'No. I am not. You've definitely got the wrong number.' She cut the call. Ten seconds later it rang again. 'See, not the wrong number. I've got the card right here in front of me. It says . . .'

Viv was spitting mad by now. 'I don't care what it says. It's the wrong number.'

He laughed again. A forced laugh without mirth. 'Someone's trying to set you up then. Vivacious Vivian will look after your every need. Come now, give her a ring. That's what it says, clear as day.'

'So, if you do have a card with my number on it, where did you find it?'

'There was a pile of them in the phone booth of . . .' He stopped speaking. She heard a train slowing then a voice making an announcement over a tannoy. He was in the Waverley station. She hesitated but then decided it was worth a try. She grabbed her keys, locked up still holding onto the phone with the noise of the station in the background, jogged up Victoria Street, over the High Street and down the steps at the side of the bank which led to the Waverley Bridge. Less than five minutes and she was on her way down the steep hill to the station's concourse.

She tried to keep her voice steady as she ran. 'Hello, hello. Where are you? I'll come to you.' If there was a pile of these about, she had to get her hands on them before anyone else did. She scanned the space, but it was heaving with people rushing to and from platforms. How was she going to identify him? He hadn't hung up but hadn't answered her either. She listened to the noises from her phone and followed them into the undercover sitting area where the tickets were sold. She scanned the room. There wasn't a single male who stood out. But there was one, about fiftyish, wearing a dark suit and a fake tan, slumped on a bench with his phone in his hand. As she approached she realised something was wrong. His head was slightly hanging onto his shoulder. She shouted into her phone and heard her own voice coming from his hand. She cut her side of the call and said, 'Hello, hello, are you okay?' She stood right in front of him. His eyes were closed. He had passed out, his phone in one hand and a bright pink card in the other. Her head had been Photoshopped onto an amazing body.

'Holy shit! She grabbed the card, slipped it into her pocket and touched the man's wrist to check for a pulse. There was one, but it was faint. She dialled 999 and asked for an ambulance. She explained what she'd seen and the operator asked if she could remain with him. 'Yes. I can stay.'

She took out the card and, sure enough, it was her number and there was no mistaking that her face was there on top of a female body, the likes of which she'd never seen in nature. Breasts like melons and abs like a washboard, not to mention a waistline that she could slip one hand round and have her fingers meet. If it wasn't so serious, she'd be laughing. Where the hell had he found it and how many were in circulation? Luckily this was the first call that she'd had. With any luck they hadn't been around long. One or two people glanced at the man as they passed but no one stopped to offer help. She held him upright on the bench as he began to slide to one side. She switched his phone off. The last thing she needed was for him to be whisked away in an ambulance and her phone to be blocked by his open call. She looked around. Most folks were distracted by their phones, or the announcements board. She took the risk to check his pockets. His wallet had credit cards in the name of William Wallace. Someone was having a laugh. She found his driving licence, same name. Surely a pseudonym or he'd been born to the parents from hell. Within a few minutes she heard the siren of an ambulance approaching, then paramedics trotted across the concourse. He was all theirs now. She told them how she'd found him and decided against going in the ambulance with him. She didn't wish him ill but she had what she needed.

She fingered the card in her pocket as she made her way back up the steep slope to Waverley Bridge. It was glossy and bigger than a business card. Anyone could have had these made and dumped them as a prank. But why? What did they have to gain, apart from her getting annoying phone calls? So far only one call, so not a huge demand for sex with women who look like super-heroines. She looked at the image again, it was laughable. No woman looked like that apart from in a Marvel comic strip, but someone had gone to a bit of trouble with Photoshop.

Her phone rang. 'Hey Mac, how're you doing?'

'Fine, Vivacious Vivian.' He laughed.

'Oh my God! How the hell do you know? In fact don't even go there. I just had a call from a guy who happened to be close enough for me to track down.'

'Lucky for you DS Nicholson was working on a case in the High Street and recognised you on one of the cards up on a board at the side of the telephone. Who knew that pubs still had landlines? Anyway she scooped up the card and had a scout round and found a few more. She had the sense to send her PC up the High Street to search every pub, loo cubicle and telephone booth from Holyrood to the Castle to gather any that she could find. You should check the pubs in the Grassmarket. Any idea who'd have done it?'

'No. It seems like an awful lot of bother to tarnish my name. I suppose it could be related to the silent calls. They're a nuisance, and calls from desperate people wanting sex would be too.'

'You seem to be taking this rather well. I'd be furious if someone did that to me. It's libellous, and a miracle that DS Nicholson is as on the ball as she is.'

'You're right, it is a miracle. But aren't you being a tad precious?' She laughed. 'I'm grateful it was Red that found it and knew what to do. I owe her big time. Now the only hassle is I'll have to change my number.'

'Actually on that subject, the NTF want everyone to use a special line. You're going to be issued with a special phone the next time you're in.'

Viv perked up. 'I like the sound of a "special phone". What will it do that others don't? Apart from be able to track our every move.'

'Not much. We can track your other phone pretty easily these days anyway. You wouldn't use the NTF one for any other business.'

'Fair enough. I'm amazed it's taken them this long. Look, where is Red? I could try and catch up with her.'

'She's back here at Fettes. I'll pass on your thanks.'

'I bet the whole office has had a good laugh?'

'Actually, she brought them all straight to me. She'd definitely got your back. You don't need to worry – we've shredded them. Well, not all of them, since I thought we might want to have one analysed, check them for prints – you never know, we might get lucky.'

'I've got one of my own. There's nothing about the text that gives anything away.'

'We could have the paper and ink analysed if you like? They had quite a few printed.'

'Shit. You think there are a lot more out there?'

'If I were them I'd do the cheapest print run. The more you print the cheaper it is. There could be a thousand.'

She groaned. 'Right, I'd better get moving and start on the pubs round the Grassmarket and the West Port. It could take a while. By the way, the guy that rang me had some kind of seizure or fainted. He had to be taken away in an ambulance.'

'What? You tell me that now? We need to speak to him.'

'He clearly wasn't interested in sex. Wasn't capable of it. He was taunting me. I took the card out of his hand. It's well thumbed. But the fact that he's the only person to have rung me indicates that it's not been around very long or that no one is interested in having sex with a cartoon character.'

'I wouldn't be too hasty about that. Go check those pubs near you, and I'll see if I can find out who your man is.'

'Oh, his name is, wait for it, William Wallace.'

He sighed. 'And you know this how?'

'I had a look in his pockets. Found a wallet.'

'What else did you find?'

'Nothing of interest.'

'I don't believe that for a second.' Mac sighed. 'You'll let me know when it suits you.'

'Right, I'm off to those pubs. I'll call if I find anything.'

Chapter Thirty

She squinted as she left daylight behind and entered the gloom of the Black Bull. She headed straight for the gents' loo. In the interest of decorum she shouted, 'Anyone here?' But when no one answered she sidled in and scanned the cubicles. The walls were clean. She then checked the small phone booth where she did actually spot an edge of the infamous pink background sticking out beneath another card selling someone's wares. She pulled the card out and sure enough, 'Vivacious Viv' was looking as desirable as root canal treatment. She checked the floor and made a quick exit. No one could spend a second longer in there than they needed to. She saw a tattered local phone directory tied to the wall next to the payphone. She gave it a shake just in case they'd been stuffed inside. Nothing. Was there still a use for a pay phone? Even newbie criminals bought burner phones that they could dispose of. As she made her way to the exit she spotted a man sitting on his own, a face she recognised, the man from the photograph that her mum had pointed out. He stared right at her then nodded to the seat opposite him. He looked as if he was drinking water but it could just have easily been a half pint of vodka or gin. She pulled the chair out and sank onto it.

He said, 'My name is Francis Muldoon.'

She smiled. 'You already know who I am so I'll spare you the pleasantries.' She held up the card. Are you responsible for this?'

He shook his head. 'No, not my style any more.'

She snorted. 'Reformed, are you?'

'You could say that.' He unwrapped a scarf that was tied round his neck, exposing a dog-collar.

'You in fancy dress?'

He smiled. 'I knew this was a shot in the dark. I thought I might be able to help you, but if you're going to be difficult . . .'

She leaned back in her seat. 'Difficult is my default setting, especially with strangers. You should ask my mum.' There was not the flicker of an eye at the mention of her mum, so not the person who'd left the note at her sheltered housing complex?

He laid a hand on the table-top. 'I know you've been looking into my family.'

'And how would you know that?'

He pointed to his collar. 'This opens many doors. My family are rather defensive about anyone poking around in their business.'

'And you've been sent to warn me off?'

'Not exactly. I heard rumblings and, as you know, I also witnessed the theft from the Range Rover the other day. I saw you chase . . .' He hesitated, not naming the person she'd apprehended. 'I heard your father was one of my dad's adversaries.'

'I heard that too. Any idea what went on?'

'My dad thought that your dad was a bit of a spoilsport; wouldn't leave him alone to get on with his job. Threats were made. I think it might have got physical.'

She stared at him. 'But my dad was on the right side of the law.' More of a question than a statement.

He tilted his head to one side. 'My dad thought the boundary between legal and illegal was a fine, sometimes blurred, one.'

'And my dad had more clarity and wasn't prepared to cross the boundary, blurred or not?'

He stared at her through the most amazing dark eyes framed by enviable lashes. More like a Hollywood version of a priest than a real one. He said, 'We each have versions of our dads that we've built over time. Probably not the most accurate representation of who they really were but we'll go a long way to protect memories that we believe in. But we're having some family squabbles at the moment and one of my brothers is digging up dirt. He thinks he's found a score that wasn't settled, only his view mind, so he's determined to put that right. He's trying to look tougher than he is and doesn't care whose cage he rattles in the process. There's a chance that it will all be settled in-house as it were, but I discovered he'd hired someone to make those.' He nodded to the pink card she still had in her hand. 'I guessed he'd heard about the theft going badly and your name was one that he had already come across. Trust me, he's not a nice man and those are just the beginning.' He gestured to the card again.

'I'm on it. There's nothing that you've said that I didn't already know.'

He sighed. 'Although you might not know that our dads knew each other as kids. I don't think they were ever best mates but I have a photograph of a group of young boys who'd been playing football on the street. I think one of them is your dad.'

She sat up. 'Have you got it on you?'

He slipped his hand inside his coat and pulled out a black and white photograph and handed it to her. She scanned the faces and the street. The tenements in the background were definitely on the street where her dad had lived. The light in the pub was so poor, she said, 'Can I take it to the door? I can't see properly.'

He nodded. 'Sure.'

She went to the door of the pub and swung it open. She couldn't take her eyes off the photograph. Was it possible that her dad had known the notorious Muldoon? As kids they'd never have understood what the other would become, but it put a different spin on how they were with each other. She ran her finger over the face of the young boy who became her dad. He'd come from such a different world to the one he'd created for her mum and his children. He must have been determined to find a way out of poverty. If he'd still been around, he'd be horrified that she'd even thought he'd come from poverty. Her grannie, her dad's mum, was fond of saying that being well off was relative since there was always someone who had less than them. She didn't want to go back inside and have to give up the photograph, but she did. She handed it back but he shook his head. 'You can keep it – I have another copy.'

She hesitated, then put her hand with the photograph against her heart. 'Thanks. I don't have many pictures of him when he was young. I don't suppose many people had cameras in those days. Not like now.' She put the photograph inside her rucksack. 'Thanks again. But what are we to do about your brother?'

He smiled. 'Good. So you accept that I'm not your enemy.'

'You probably already know that a gift isn't simply the transfer of an object. It's an alliance. If I still saw you as an enemy I wouldn't have accepted it. So what about this brother of yours?'

He shifted in his seat and leaned forward on the table. 'I think he has his eye . . .'

Viv interrupted. 'My mum?'

He nodded slowly. 'And your sister.'

'Why are you telling me? Won't this put you in an unfavourable position?'

'As I indicated, I'm now a fully paid-up man of the cloth. Different boss now.' He sipped his water or whatever it was. 'Can I get you a drink?'

She shook her head, unable to work him out. Was he genuinely trying to help? What other agenda could he have? 'So, what's in this for you?'

'I've been trying to reduce the violence. There's no need for it. People can be damaged in far more long-lasting ways than giving them a black eye or knocking a few teeth out. That's where you come in. I know that you work for the NTF, so they must think you're pretty good at something. They normally keep outsiders well away. I've got a notion that we could be mutually beneficial.'

She pushed her hair off her face. 'I'm not sure what you're on about. I'm a hairdresser.'

He laughed. 'I heard you give a lecture once and you never once mentioned hair, but you did mention never underestimating your audience.'

She blew out a breath. 'You took classes at New College? Or George Square?'

'Did a few religious studies electives. Can't be a convincing priest if you know nothing of other faiths. Even Freudianism.'

She raised her eyebrows. 'You run that by your bishop yet?'

To his credit he smiled. 'Not yet.'

With the smile his face softened, changing from foe to potential friend in a few muscles. There was no denying his good looks. She imagined they caused all manner of issues in his parish. His straight white teeth, strong square jaw, high cheekbones, and long slender nose, not to mention a full head of dark wavy hair, all had to make him a contender for pin-up priest of the year.

She said, 'So, tell me more about your dad? I don't have much to go on since . . .'

He interrupted. 'I know he was killed in an accident . . . I mean your dad.'

She bristled and clasped her hands between her thighs.

He held up his hands. 'That was way beyond the Muldoon repertoire by the way. At that time we were on the rise from being domestic thieves to more industrial scale operations. We hadn't yet found an appetite for killing, or at least not that I knew of. I was too young to understand it all but I have some clear memories that I'd rather I didn't have.'

Her mum had mentioned that the university generation of Muldoons were a lot more to worry about than the previous ones. 'Are you the only one to go to university?'

'Goodness, no. My dad was a stickler for each of us getting an education before we branched out.' He smiled again. 'Not that he wanted us to branch out beyond the family firm. But he believed that education was the only thing that couldn't be taken from you. Ironic really.'

'How did he react to your becoming a priest?'

'He was resigned, as if he realised someone had to take one for the team and I was that someone. I think he quite admired it. I was there to serve him his last rites. He seemed to find that amusing. I have five brothers and a sister so there were plenty of others to do his bidding, but he asked for me at the end.'

'Had you fallen out?'

He tilted his head. 'Well let's say we'd agreed to differ. Power and greed are addictive. He'd lost his way.'

'Which one has it in for me?'

'Sean. He's always been short of attention and didn't care whether it was negative attention or not as long as he got it. He mistakenly believes that he's doing an honourable thing getting at you. But I understand that my dad and yours were kind of, I'm not sure what you'd call it because it sure wasn't friendship, but, you know that saying, "honour among thieves"?'

She nodded. 'My dad wasn't a thief though.'

'No, I know that, but he did understand that there was a code of conduct which, as long as it didn't cross a certain line, was tolerated. My dad originally made his money from taking things that people had put out for rubbish. Cleaning up other people's muck. He'd find a buyer or he'd break them up and sell the parts. He saw it as a social service. Your dad knew, but didn't mind even though it was still theft. The streets were tidier.' He sighed and shook his head. 'He'd had a tough childhood, didn't want us to have to scrimp for stuff. My mum did her best but, like I said, power and greed are addictive and also aphrodisiacs. Once he started straying my mum just kept her head down.' He'd been staring at his hands clasped round his glass on the table but looked up. 'You're a good listener.'

She stared at him. It was rare for her to meet anyone with stories about her dad. She was hungry to hear anything that reconnected her to the living, breathing dad that she didn't have. Could he be trusted? 'Why are you really here?'

'I watch Sean going down routes that would have our dad turning in his grave but Sean thinks he'd be proud. He doesn't get it. He doesn't get the code of honour. All he wants is power, money and to make sure Mark, the brother that is his bet noir, doesn't become regarded as the head of the family. Mark knows the business and the code. Sean's getting into some seriously petty stuff.' He pointed to the pink card she still held in her hand. 'You sure you won't have a drink?'

'D'you know what? I think I will.'

He went to stand.

'No, you're all right, I'll get it. You want a top-up?'

'I wouldn't mind, this is warm with me holding onto it. Fizzy water with lemon and ice.'

She grinned. 'Saving yourself for the communion wine?'

He gave a half laugh and she loped off to the bar. There was only one barman on duty and his eyes were glued to a game of golf on the TV. She cleared her throat. He came to her but kept one eye on the screen.

'What can I get you?' Still staring at the screen.

'Two glasses of fizzy water, one with ice and lemon, the other neat.'

As he poured the water from a hose on the bar she said, 'You know the padre over there?'

He glanced towards Muldoon. 'Been in a few times recently but he's not a known regular.'

Interesting. Why wouldn't bar staff categorise the people that they served into groups? 'Known regulars' was a good one. At least the padre wasn't in the, 'this one's trouble' group.

'Does the collar raise eyebrows?'

The barman laughed. 'You're kidding me. Our busiest time of year is when the General Assembly is on. Can hardly get a seat. Wall-to-wall dog-collars.'

'I suppose caring for souls is more difficult than we think.'

'Aye. It must be.'

She tapped her bank card against the machine and returned to the table with the drinks.

Father Muldoon said, 'I bet he hears just as many confessions as I do.'

'Where's your parish?'

'I'm just about to start as a chaplain at the University of Edinburgh.'

She raised her eyebrows. 'Nice tender souls away from home, been warned to keep the faith.' She sipped her drink. 'In my experience, by second year, most students have had enough of hangovers and waking up with strangers and they're keen to get their act together. That's when they'll seek out your help, return to your fold.'

'I'm not sure how it'll work. I've only done a locum before for a term, but I liked being in George Square and I like having access to New College library.'

New College was her comfort zone. She'd done most of her degrees there and enjoyed that it was collegiate. 'It's certainly more peaceful than the main library and the librarians know everyone by name, so it's harder to eat crisps or use your phone.'

'Now that you say it out loud I think that's exactly why I like it.'

'So, Sean's the thorn in the family's side?'

'No one's ever said that but he's the one who is giving me most concern. The nuisance calls to you, the cards, the tail, those are minor, but he has escalated out of hand in the past so it could happen again. The more frustrated he gets the more he loses it.'

'How do you know that he's been tailing me?'

'I'm not the only brother who can sense he's getting out of hand and my sister doesn't like what she's seeing either. But she's loyal; she'll talk to me but she'd never talk to anyone who isn't family about things she's worried about. And trust me, she's worried.'

'You know that I'm a trained . . .'

'Analyst? Yes. I enjoyed your lectures and I took lots of notes. We have a lot in common. More in common than the things you think divide us.'

'Well, I think you'll find that I come from a family of loyal upstanding citizens who don't have the kind of rap sheet that would make Genghis Khan flip in his grave.'

He laughed. 'You can't tar us all with the same brush. It's not genetic. I've found a way out.'

'You wouldn't be the first corrupt clergyman I've known. What do you want from me?'

'I don't think I want anything apart from the satisfaction of Sean not getting his own way.'

'Hard for me to believe that. Although, families, eh, who'd have them?'

His hands reminded her of Mac's – long fingers, short manicured nails. She had a thing about clean nails. He passed the test. She wondered if he played the piano. 'You don't play the piano, do you?'

His eyebrows knitted together. 'Funny you should ask. I've been learning the organ. Scrambles my brain but that means I can't think about anything else. Good therapy.'

'You must have someone that you can offload to?'

He took a long draw on his drink. Ice clinked against the sides of the glass. 'I'm not sure that the church has got the hang of support for their staff yet. Cure of souls is to be administered by me, not received.' He glanced up as the door to the pub swung open and let in a shaft of light.

She turned and looked at who had entered. 'You waiting for someone?'

He shook his head. 'No, I've been waiting for you. Struck lucky today. I guessed that once you got wind of those cards you'd be on the hunt. It made sense that you'd look close to home so I took my chances here.'

She drained her glass. 'Well, I'm not sure where we go from here, Father Muldoon.'

'Call me Francis.'

'Do the family call you Francis?'

'Yes. Never Frank or Frankie. Although a couple of tutors tried it as a befriending thing, but it didn't work. Odd what's in a name.'

'Have you any idea how many of these cards are out there?'

'I don't but I'll find out and let you know.'

She handed him one of her own cards. 'You don't need to hang about in bars on the off-chance that we'll meet. Give me a ring. I'm going round the rest of the local pubs to retrieve as many as I can.' She stood and turned towards the door.

As if he was reluctant for her to leave he said, 'We're almost neighbours now.'

She turned back. 'How come?'

'The university have given me the use of a flat in George Square. We'll probably bump into each other. Or,' he grinned, 'you could come to one of my services.'

She walked to the door and looked back. He raised his glass and nodded. She liked him, so reminded herself to be wary. It was easy to be taken in by the collar but, as she'd said, she had encountered dodgy clergy before and his lineage didn't bode well for him.

Chapter Thirty-One

She strode into the White Hart Inn still smiling and carried out the same check that she had in the Black Bull. Sean, or whoever the lackey was who'd delivered the cards on his behalf, had done a thorough job. When people do thorough jobs they do it out of respect or fear. For this she'd put money on fear. Every bar that she went into she found at least one card which meant either they hadn't left too many in each or they'd already been lifted, which could mean she'd be in for a load of phone calls if she didn't get her number changed asap. After the Grassmarket she did the pubs on Candlemaker Row, George IV Bridge and Forrest Road, and as a final just-in-case she jogged along in front of the old Royal Infirmary building, now posh flats, then down the side of the Art College to the West Port. Every pub had cards with her face on them. She returned to the West Bow, nipped into the Bow Bar and found one in the gents' loo. There was no way she'd got them all but she had to get as many as possible.

Frustrated and flustered, she exited the Bow Bar at a rate of knots and bumped into a woman. She apologised and looked up into the woman's face. 'Oh, hello. You're the vet from Doune.'

The woman, equally flustered, said, 'Yes. Yes I am a vet from Doune. And you are Sal Chapman's friend.'

Viv nodded. 'What brings you to Edinburgh?'

'I've just sneaked out from a conference up at the uni. I'm looking for a birthday gift for my mum. And the last speaker was deadly dull. How is Mollie?'

Viv smiled. 'She's great. But I think she misses Sal.'

The woman nodded. 'We all miss Sal.'

Viv stared at the ground. She had met this woman in the loo after Sal's memorial service and something in their conversation then made her think she and Sal had had something going beyond her being Moll's vet. That same feeling washed over her standing on the pavement outside her flat.

'Look, I'd better get going. I'll no doubt see you and Mollie sometime in Doune.'

'Yes. No doubt. Hope you find a gift.' Viv watched the woman continue up Victoria Street until she crossed the road and went into the second-hand bookshop.

As she put her key into the lock of the flat her mobile rang. Silence. She said, 'Fuck off.' And cut the call. Time to do some call tracing. Once inside her office under the eaves she began a search. There was no way of doing this legally but too bad. If Sean Muldoon thought he could intimidate her with the kind of stuff he'd done so far he was sadly mistaken. She prepared to interrupt his game. There was no point in being a seasoned hacker if she couldn't apply her skills when she needed them.

As she booted up, her phone rang again, but this time it was Mac. 'Hey. How are you doing?'

'Fine, the cards were made by . . .'

She stopped him. 'I was just thinking about ringing you. It's a guy called Sean Muldoon who put the cards out. He's also the one who's been calling and tailing me.'

'Wow, that was quick work.'

'I got lucky and met his brother, Father Francis Muldoon, in the Black Bull of all places. He wants to help. I'm just about to put a spanner in Sean's works. And before you ask how, don't.'

She up-ended her rucksack and a flurry of pink cards fell onto her desk. 'I've got about fifty cards here. He's not going to like what . . . actually delete that. Shit! What now? Hang on, there's someone trying to bang my door down.' She marched up her hall and looked through the spy hole. Whoever was on the other side had his or her finger over it. 'Mac, I'll have to go.'

'Don't do anything stupid. I'll call you back in five to make sure you're okay.'

She put the chain over and secured it, then slowly opened the door. Two men in dark suits stood with their hands behind their backs and their legs apart.

One asked, 'Are you Dr Vivian Fraser?' The other, the taller of the two, pulled out a wallet with ID.

Viv glanced at it. 'To what do I owe this pleasure?'

'We want to have a word about your online activity.'

She snorted. 'Good luck with that. It seems to me you're out of your jurisdiction.'

'We only want to have a word.'

'Sure. You think I came up the Clyde . . .' She saw the confusion on their faces and said, 'Forget it. I'm busy.'

The tall one stepped forward so she quickly pushed the door closed and rang Mac. His number went to voicemail. He'd ring back soon. When he said five minutes he meant it. She stood behind the door and didn't see either of the men make a move to go. True to form her phone rang again. 'Hey, Mac, you'll never guess who is on the other side on my door.'

'No, you're right, I won't, so tell me.'

'The FBI.'

'Why on earth would the FBI come to your home?'

She hesitated. 'I've been . . .'

He interrupted. 'God, Viv, what did I tell you? There's no way they'll give anything up. Our top intelligence guys are still on it. You must have been interfering. I'd have thought they'd have come to us first. What exactly have you done?'

'Nothing that shouldn't have been done in order to find out what really happened to Sal.' She heard him take in a breath.

'Look, ask them to make contact with the NTF. I'll go and see the boss right now. See what we can do. Are they still at the door?'

'Yes, but the door is shut.'

'Not very hospitable, are you.'

'I didn't realise they'd come for tea. I'll tell them, but don't go to Ruddy yet. Stay on the line.'

She opened the door a crack and one of the agents stuck his foot in the gap.

She said, 'It's in everyone's interest for you to speak to my colleague at the NTF. I'll put him on speaker.'

Mac said, 'This is DCI Marconi from the NTF. I think there's been some misunderstanding.'

One of the agents pointed a pen-shaped tool at her phone and it went dead. 'What the fu**?'

She kicked his toes and slammed the door shut. When she tried to get her phone going again nothing happened. She went to her landline and rang Mac. Without any preamble she said, 'They used a device on my mobile to knock it out.'

'Are they still there?'

'I don't know, wait I'll check.' When she looked through the spy hole there was no sign of anyone. She opened the door a crack and heard footsteps receding down the stairwell. 'They're leaving.'

'I'm not sure they have the right to use that device on a UK operative.' He sighed. 'Just how illegal was your search?'

'As I've said, nothing that we shouldn't be doing to find out what happened. There's no way you or I or anyone else should let this go. We've got to find out.'

'I agree, but we have to do it properly. We've been over this, Viv.'

'Yes, and by the time we do it pro-per-ly, they'll have buried every scrap of evidence they ever had.'

'Despite what you think, you are not the only person who has creative cyber skills. This enquiry is being done at top level. Stuff like that doesn't happen overnight. It's multi-agency. Please leave it to us for now. I'm begging you.'

She blew out a breath. 'For now, but no promises for the long term.'

'I'll go and speak to the boss. There's bound to be something in his inbox that I haven't yet heard about. I'll speak to you later. But in the meantime do me a favour and keep yourself busy poking around in our west coast project.'

She closed the door of her office and stared at the desktop screen. It was more tempting to go poking around the Quantico and FBI servers, but she hesitated. She didn't want to force them to delete info any more than she probably had already. She settled down and began investigating the Irish estate or farm. What would they call it? Whatever they were up to would have left some trail that she could uncover on the net or on their mobiles, but she needed her own mobile to do that and the FBI guy had scuppered that. She retrieved her mobile phone, switched it off and on again. Nothing. 'Shit.' She thought about the device the FBI guy had just used. Did they have these tucked away in the stores of the basement at NTF HQ? She made a mental note to have a look next time she was in the building. Whatever the Americans were up to the Brits were often ahead, although more discreet about it. She raked around in the bottom drawer of her desk. She'd hoped she wouldn't have to use it but she kept a spare phone for emergencies and this was an emergency. The SIM card from the dead phone worked when she transferred it, which was interesting since it meant that the device that had been used to knock it out was attacking the battery. Checking that would have to wait, as would finding out whoever Sean Muldoon had delegated to be the persistent silent caller. She knew it was a Muldoon goon, but which one? If they'd wanted to do anything more than bug her they probably would have before now? She wasn't convinced, but for now she had other fish to fry.

She leaned back on her chair and rubbed her eyes. Staring at Google Earth was certainly taking its toll. She decided that a cup of tea and a biscuit was in order, and as she wandered up the hall she smiled at the sound of music coming from Ronnie's flat. It was unlike him to have the volume up as loud as it was, but she reminded herself to be grateful for his almost invisible presence. She stared out of the kitchen window and admired the Heriots buildings all lit up and the dark bulk of the old Infirmary now converted into grand flats. Nowhere ever stays the same; even a city like Edinburgh, steeped in history, had to change. She flinched at a loud knock on her door. She glanced at her phone, 10pm, a bit late for visitors. She opened the door to the tall men in dark suits holding up their FBI badges.

'What now?'

'We have some of Ms Chapman's belongings. We'd like you to identify them.'

'It is Doctor Chapman. And why would you want me to do that this late in the game?'

'The belongings were in evidence, taken from the car . . .'

'Why didn't you bring them here?'

'We are not certified to take them from US soil.'

'What, so you think I'm coming all the way to the USA to look through a handbag that may or may not belong to her?'

'Well, it's only a five-minute drive to the consulate, which is US soil.'

The one who abstained from speaking moved from foot to foot. She didn't trust them, but it couldn't do any harm to go to the consulate if it would get them off her case. 'Okay, I'll do it. But you have to back off. Stop using your crazy intimidation tactics; they are so last year.'

The taller agent raised his eyebrows. 'You'd surely want to know if these are Doctor Chapman's things or not?' He stressed the title.

'Don't be facetious, she earned that title.' She snatched up her jacket, phone and keys. 'Okay, let's go.'

Chapter Thirty-Two

The woman huffed and puffed but eventually handed her pinkish-gold mobile phone to Viv. So grateful, she didn't even raise an eyebrow at the woman's long glittery nails. Her brown uniform was a sign that she was a member of support staff. Viv slipped inside the toilet cubicle and rang Mac's number.

It rang and rang and just when she thought it was going to voicemail he picked up. 'Hello, this is a private number.'

'Mac, it's me, Viv. I need your help.' He was about to interrupt but she said, 'It's urgent. I'm at the old Turnhouse Airport, about to be put on a plane to the US against my will. Those two FBI suits are waiting outside the loos. They don't like me much. I've borrowed someone's phone. You have to help. If they get me to the US . . .'

'Okay, okay. Slow down. Which building are you in?'

'I don't know. We entered by the Old Turnhouse Road. I'm in a building that's for cargo flights. All I could see were planes without windows and not a passenger in sight. D'you think you can do something?' She bit down on her lip. If anyone could do something to help it was Mac.

She heard him typing on another phone.

'I'm on it. There's a guy that I used to work with on the security team there. I'll see if I can get hold of him.'

The woman banged on the cubicle door. 'Look, I need my phone back. I have to go.'

'Yeah, sorry, be right out. Mac, you've got to do something.'

'What were you doing? In fact, don't answer that.'

The woman banged on the door again.

'Okay. Okay.' Viv came out and handed over the phone. 'Thank you, thank you, that was a life saver.'

The woman raised her super-sculpted eyebrows and stomped off. 'Whatever!'

Viv washed her hands and threw cold water on her face. Then took her time drying up. Every minute she could stall in the loo was time for Mac to get help. One of the suits banged on the door. She jumped and in the hope of keeping them from getting too angry she opened the door. They were standing on either side.

The taller said, 'Everything okay?'

Viv shrugged. They marched in a row towards a cubicle marked Passport Control. The guy who was the taller raised some kind of badge and the man behind the glass held up his hand to prevent them from going through.

The US agent said, 'We're covered. Ring your boss. They've given us the okay.'

'Sorry sir, I have orders to stop all foreign security.'

'But we've been cleared.' He looked angry.

The man behind the glass glanced at Viv. 'Do you have a passport, ma'am?'

Viv shook her head. 'No, not with me.'

The passport control officer began shuffling papers on his desk inside the little glass cube. Viv recognised his actions as someone stalling for time. She noticed his shoulders drop with relief and she looked behind her. Another official-looking man trotted across the concourse.

The newcomer said, 'Follow me,' and led them to a room with a lock on the door that required a number to be keyed in. The linoleum flooring, metal table and chairs, and strip lighting looked like prison issue. They were given polystyrene cups of horrible weak coffee and asked to wait until another official, who would hopefully seal Viv's fate, arrived. The agents had told the guy at passport security that she was with them of her own accord, which wasn't entirely true since they'd made some threats, but not having a passport was a legitimate reason for anyone on the control desk to prevent her from travelling. Mac must have managed to get to his friend. The agents paced and asserted their masculinity with hideous machismo posturing, their legs apart, jackets open, hands on hips, pushing out their family planning. If the FBI didn't invest in a bit more psych training, it would continue to function like a bad fifties cop movie.

Eventually a woman entered and said, 'I'm sorry, but we can't let this woman travel unless she has a valid passport.'

Both men opened their mouths to protest but the woman silenced them with a raised hand. 'Not my call. We have one rule for all. No passport no travel, unless you have an extradition order.'

The agents looked at each other, then the taller one spoke, 'We were supposed to be covered.' He took out his phone and looked at the screen.

'Well sadly that is misinformation. She isn't going anywhere.'

He typed a text message into his phone. 'We'll see.'

The woman nodded. 'Can I get you anything?'

Viv said to the agents, 'I'd like my phone back.'

Again one looked at the other. They both shrugged. The shorter guy retrieved her phone from his inside pocket and handed it to her.

She rang Mac on speed-dial.

'Viv. You okay?'

'Yeah. I don't suppose.'

'I'm about fifteen minutes away. We'll get this sorted out. How heavy-handed were they?'

'Not very. I'll tell you when I see you.'

The agent kept looking at his phone but whatever he was expecting didn't happen. They continued to pace and exhale, going for maximum intimidation. Viv thought it was funny but didn't laugh. Making a bad situation worse wasn't part of her plan.

Mac arrived and asked for Viv to be taken to another room. The woman led her to a room with carpets and comfortable seats, the opposite of the musty austere room they'd left.

'This is better.'

'I'm not going to ask what you've done to deserve the strings that Marconi has pulled to make this happen. But you should be eternally grateful. If you've done something to upset the FBI then Marconi is a good man to have on your side.'

The door opened and Mac stepped in. He nodded acknowledgement to the woman then said, 'You want to tell me what's been going on?'

Viv hung her head. 'It's a long story and I'm sure you can guess it. I had to try to find out. I couldn't let it lie. I couldn't let her die and not do everything possible to uncover the whole story.'

'So, what? You hacked into Quantico? I told you they'd be tracking anybody who was too interested in . . .'

'I know what you said. What would you have done?'

He ran his hands through his hair and it stood on end. The gesture was so familiar to Viv and she wanted to fix it, push it back into place. But resisted.

'You will have to speak to them.'

'They can't have traced it back to me. They're still fishing.'

'They have the most sophisticated system in the Western world. You think they can't trace one little hacker?'

'They haven't. There's no way I'd have left a trail that they could find. Every time I . . .'

Mac held up his hand. 'Don't.' He whipped his hand across his throat in a slashing gesture and mouthed, 'Not here.' Then raised his voice. 'Are you willing to answer their questions?'

'Yes, if you stay in the room with me.'

'I'm not sure they'll buy that, but I'll ask.'

He left.

The woman said, 'As I said, you must be worth a great deal to him. Our relations with the USA have never been more fragile. The tiniest thing could make that a whole lot worse. He's taking a risk.'

Viv nodded. 'Yes, I get it. I owe him big time, but I don't think this is a matter of national security.'

The woman shot Viv a how-would-you-know look but said, 'I'm sure you'll make it up to him.'

Viv was about to put her right on the nature of their relationship but realised she was unable to define it herself. Was it mutual? They'd both got each other's backs but this time Mac was out on a limb for her.

Mac returned. 'They've agreed, with some resistance, to me being in the room when they question you. Let's go. This needn't take long.'

Viv was right; they were on a fishing expedition with no solid proof that she had hacked into their system, although she sensed they were getting warmer. They had to relinquish her, but from the way that the taller one stared at her he wasn't done with her yet. She shrugged and nodded to him. 'I guess that's us then?'

He shot back. 'I wouldn't bank on it, lady.'

She was about to remind him that she had no aspirations to be a lady but bit her lip and turned away from him before she said something she'd regret. Mac tapped her arm and gestured her to come with him.

On the drive home she explained to Mac exactly what she'd been doing, but without compromising her partners or their sites. 'I couldn't not search. I can't believe that the FBI didn't do a major cover-up of Sal's death. It was all sorted too quickly. Too conveniently. But who benefited from that?'

'I understand why you'd want to pursue it your own way, but how many times do I have to spell it out? We've got a team of guys on it. You should speak to them.'

'Why? You think they'll tell me anything?'

'Of course. They know that you're with us.'

She let out a huge sigh. 'Sometimes it's not in my interest to be so independent. Thanks, by the way. I really do owe you.'

'You sure do.' He winked. 'Occasionally it would help if you trusted me. Kept me in the loop. But mostly you do good work with us. Team player or not, you're an asset and the guys who've been finding what happened to Sal will want you to know if they've found anything and vice versa.'

'Oh, I'm not so sure about that. Especially if I've muddied their investigation.'

'Ye of little faith. They know that you are on their side. One of these days you're going to get the hang of we're-all-in-this-together.'

'You know that I know that at some level, but at times I just . . .'

'We got you through that interview, didn't we? And we're on our way home.'

'That'll be the royal "we"? Thanks, Mac. I don't know what would have happened if I'd ended up on the other side of the Atlantic. Snowden's story didn't end well.'

Mac's head spun round to stare at her. 'Shit, you surely didn't do anything that could compare to Snowden?'

'No! But they do like to make an example of anyone who crosses them.'

'So you were crossing them?'

'Not from where I was standing. I was looking for information about how Sal managed to be seduced so quickly and whether she'd been set up before she got to the US. I got to thinking that if she'd already been corresponding with that woman there would be a trail of evidence. Or maybe the woman's lover had discovered it. Was the shooting way more premeditated than we were led to believe? You knew Sal better, well certainly for longer, than I did. She began the affair too quickly after she arrived. That was completely out of character. You believe that whatever she was doing it was to maintain her cover, don't you?'

'Sal was no cheater, so it didn't add up that she'd got involved with someone so soon. Unless there was a really good reason.'

Viv heaved a sigh, rubbed her face then ran her hands through her hair. 'Can we talk about something else? How about food? Are you hungry?'

'Funny you should mention that. There's rarely a time when I couldn't be persuaded to eat. Bella's?'

'Yes please . . .' She rubbed her hands over her face again. 'That was surreal. It's not every day that the FBI turn up at my door, never mind ask me to accompany them. You know they took me to the consulate first. Impressive security there now. Double body scanners at the entrance. That's how they got hold of my phone. After a few questions there they asked me to go with them. They took me in a car with full diplomatic plates and all, but they were vague about where we were going. As soon as we started heading out of town I started to worry. There's no consulate in the west – we had to be headed somewhere else. The rest you know. Surely they can't just do that?'

'They didn't abduct you. You went willingly.'

'Yes. But my willingness didn't extend to getting on a flight to the US. They missed that bit out.'

'Worry not. I'll get someone to look into it. I'm just glad you're okay and they didn't rough you up.'

'That would've been risky. As you know I'm not exactly calm in a physical crisis.'

He smirked. 'I think you usually do well in a crisis otherwise you wouldn't be any good to us. I mean, compared to some people, you're positively horizontal.'

Now she knew he was taking the piss. 'I'm not that bad.'

'You carrying your Gerber?'

'Yeah. It's wrapped inside my sanitary protection. Got to rely on the embarrassment of men. Hoping that they won't start to deconstruct my large bag of pads and tampons.'

He screwed up his face. 'Clever move, I'm probably one of those guys. But now that you've given me a heads-up I'll know to make sanitary protection a search priority. By the way, you're not going to believe this, but I'm relieved you were out. There's been a fire in the West Bow.'

She turned right round to face him. 'What?'

'Some geezer set an industrial bin alight and once it was going it caught the oil left by a motor-scooter nearby. Its petrol tank exploded, which meant every possible emergency service was called in. The tyres caused enormous amounts of smoke. It was bad, but at least it wasn't another real bomb. And there's the added bonus that you were off gallivanting with the FBI.'

'Gallivanting my arse. You think the fire was an accident?'

'Not yet able to tell for sure. But every engine available was there since it was dangerously close to the stacks of the National Library.'

Viv knew those stacks. 'That would have been a disaster. Talk about a tinderbox. Although I did notice they have a swanky sprinkler system these days. Not a wet system, but some kind of powder.'

'How would you even know that? Only staff are allowed in the stacks.'

She tapped the side of her nose. 'You will never know my reach. Fingers in pies that you can only dream of.'

'Speaking of pies, or at least of food and shelter, you might not want to sleep in the flat. The place will stink of smoke. It'll take a few days to clear even with your windows wide open.'

'I've got to see Moll, so once I've had a look and packed a few things I'll head back up to Doune.'

He smiled.

'What are you grinning at?'

'Nothing.'

'Well that's even more worrying than if it was something.'

'I'm just pleased that you're less phobic about the countryside than you used to be.'

She shifted in her seat. 'I miss the dog.' She sighed. 'I love that she doesn't judge me. She's unconditionally affectionate. But you're right, I am getting used to the smell of grass. And I should really give my new outdoor study a test run. Brian assured me that it is WiFi friendly but I can't imagine it having the broadband speed that I need to . . .'

He started la-la-la-ing. 'Don't even mention whatever it is. Hacking can remain your little secret . . . I don't judge you.'

'Of course you do, it's your job. You can't let me be who I am otherwise you'd lose your job.'

'I meant outside of work.'

'You know that I don't get that work/private divide. Who or whatever I am at work is part of who I am at home and vice versa.' She glanced at him. 'My ethics are pretty consistent. Not quite Robin Hood but that's where I'd lean. I suppose that's why I'd like to find out about Sal by myself. Then I won't be in debt.'

They pulled up outside Bella's.

He said, 'Not all the world is about cheques and balances. Sometimes it's about . . .'

She interrupted him. 'I don't believe that. There's definitely no such thing as a free lunch, whether in your home or work life. However much Sal said she loved me she still kept score. I could see her frustration if I didn't do what she wanted. Oh, she always said I had a choice but the choice was to choose what she wanted.'

'God, Viv, you're an old cynic.'

She shrugged. 'Just going by experience. So when you say you don't judge me that's a lie. A white lie to yourself and to me. You wouldn't have to scrape too deep to uncover your motivation.'

He shook his head. 'I think a few more sessions in therapy would be a good idea.'

'I agree. Who do you see?'

'I didn't mean for me.'

She laughed. 'No, I thought not. Everyone could do with therapy and even that isn't unconditional, as they claim.'

He held the door for her to enter first.

'Why, thank you.'

'I hope you haven't forgotten about coming to my mum's for lunch. The sisters have been banging on at me to remind you, but I said you'd had enough on your plate this past month . . .'

'Set it up. Let's do it!'

He raised his eyebrows and slowly shook his head. 'You've no idea what you're letting yourself in for.'

Chapter Thirty-Three

Viv rummaged in her rucksack for the keys to her flat. Once inside she took the first set of stairs two at a time, but soon gave into the fatigue in her legs. As she reached the landing beneath her own she glanced up and saw a large bouquet of flowers outside her door. There was a small brown envelope addressed to 'Dr Fraser' tucked into the wrapping paper. Delivered in person then. She opened up, tossed her rucksack into the hall and lifted the flowers. This was no last-minute-garage purchase, but an exotic choice of eryngium and strelitzia with loads of fabulous spikey foliage. The card read, 'You have my word there won't be any more trouble from Sean. I hope we do bump into each other again. Or, you could always join my choir? Francis x'. She grinned. How loaded was that single handwritten cross?

The light on her answering machine blinked. Grateful that the flowers were already in a container of water she left them on her desk and pressed the button to listen to her messages. Hardly anyone apart from her mum and Jules, in desperation, used the landline number so it was no surprise to hear her mum's voice. 'Give me a ring. I can't sleep.'

She dialled and her mum picked up on the second ring. 'Hi mum, how come you can't sleep?' The Frasers had many faults but sleeplessness wasn't usually one of them.

'I was remembering how much hassle the Muldoon's caused your dad and thought the younger generation could be a lot more dangerous. You'll have to watch your back.'

'Well you can rest now. I've just had a huge bunch of flowers from Father Francis Muldoon and he assures me that I no longer have anything to worry about.'

'And you believe him?'

'Strangely enough I think I do. I met him in the pub and he talked about my dad and his and how they knew each other when they were kids.'

'I . . . wait a minute. I do remember something about that. But don't be so trusting.' Viv's eyes opened wide. Trust wasn't one of her strong suits.

'I think he's okay. He gave me a photograph of them. It's one I hadn't seen before. I'll bring it with me the next time I visit.'

'And when might that be?'

'Now that you've got your wee car you could come to Doune.'

After a moment's hesitation she said, 'I might just do that.'

Viv smiled. 'I'm going up tomorrow for a few days so no time like the present. Let me know when you're coming, but now get some sleep.'

She admired the flowers and wondered what to make of their sender. He had good taste. Who had given him access to the building? No one would deny a priest entry so it could have been anyone. The idea of singing in a choir was not the worst suggestion she'd heard, but for now she'd done enough thinking and headed to the bathroom for her night ablutions.

The End

Acknowledgements

Writing is a lonely profession, but I am not alone. My name may be on the cover but a book is a collaborative process and I am fortunate to have many collaborators, some have no idea that they contributed. I thank the anonymous woman I overheard in the queue at the supermarket. I thank Diana Campbell and Moira McPartlin who circled early drafts like buzzards homing in on my howlers. I thank my consistently fabulous editor Nicola Wood without whom I'd have lost faith at book one and who would have sliced out that 'consistently' in a beat. I thank my writers' group, my reading groups and a whole host in between. I thank my husband, Robin, who is steadfast in his support. But ultimately without you, yes you, the reader, there would be no point in writing at all, so my heartfelt thanks go to you.

Oh, and one last thing, if you've enjoyed *At Sea* there is nothing more precious to me than a review from an enthusiast, so if you have a minute.

For other books in the Viv Fraser series by V. Clifford

Visit author.to/VClifford

Printed in Great Britain
by Amazon

86251529R00113